THE CLIQUE

SUMMER COLLECTION

DYLAN

THE CLIQUE
SUMMER COLLECTION

DYLAN

A CLIQUE NOVEL BY
LISI HARRISON

poppy

LITTLE, BROWN AND COMPANY
New York   Boston

Poppy

Little, Brown and Company
Hachette Book Group USA
237 Park Avenue, New York, NY 10017
For more of your favorite series, go to www.pickapoppy.com

First Edition: May 2008

The Poppy name and logo are trademarks of Hachette Book Group USA.

Cover design by Andrea C. Uva
Cover and author photos by Roger Moenks

alloy**entertainment**

Produced by Alloy Entertainment
151 West 26th Street, New York, NY 10001

ISBN: 978-0-316-03565-1

10 9 8 7 6 5 4 3 2 1
CWO
Printed in the United States of America

For Cindy Eagan, the woman behind the curtain who makes it all happen. Buuuurp! (That was from Dylan.)

Dylan Marvil sat across from her famous TV-host mother on *The Daily Grind*'s private jet en route to a spa in Hawaii, wondering why anyone would *choose* to fly commercial. The luxe cabin was papered with interlocking D's and G's, the seats were made of butter-soft tan leather, and the in-flight movie was anything she wanted it to be. The only thing missing was a silver spoon for her fat-free triple-chocolate banana split—and the petite brunet flight attendant in the cute navy minidress was rushing one right over.

Once it had arrived, Dylan swallowed a mouthful of creamy deliciousness. "Ahhh! Brain freeze!" she shouted as the cold shot straight up to her scarlet roots.

Without lifting her emerald green eyes, Merri-Lee Marvil tossed a snowy white cashmere throw on her daughter's lap and returned to her thick file on Svetlana Slootskyia, the teen tennis phenom and current *Maxim* cover girl. Merri-Lee reclined in her seat, tucked her burgundy blowout behind her ears, and began flipping through the research material her assistant, Cassidy Wolfe, had prepared for the upcoming interview.

Until Svetlana, the only thing tennis-related Dylan had ever noticed was the sparkling diamond bracelet glinting on her mother's bony wrist. But these days, Svetlana "Tennis the Menace" Slootskyia was impossible to ignore.

At first she made headlines for her blond hotness. But then she TMZ'ed her way onto Dylan's radar when she whipped her racket at a ball girl's teeth after losing a majorly important match. And this was only four days after she'd smashed her now-ex-boyfriend in the mouth with a Dunlop because he smile-thanked the soda girl for his Pepsi. After twelve weeks of anger-management therapy, Svetlana had emerged to scores of paparazzi, all of them hoping to snap *her* the instant she snapped again.

Now, every entertainment journalist from Maria Menounos to Nancy O'Dell was tripping over their Manolos to get a post-rehab interview with Svetlana. But she was more impossible to land than Chanel's Black Tulip nail polish, thanks to Merri-Lee, who'd bought the rights to the Slootskyia story the second Svetlana's Wilson KFactor collided with Ali Chipley's incisors.

"Ha! I'll show *her*," Merri-Lee blurted, scribbling something on her yellow legal pad.

"Who?" Dylan licked the silver dessert spoon and dropped it in the fat-free chocolate soup that was starting to congeal at the bottom of her crystal bowl.

"Barbara Walters. She's not the only one willing to go *there*."

It was the interview of the season, and Merri-Lee was determined to deliver high drama. But to Dylan, Svetlana represented a first-class ticket to a five-star fat camp, an opportunity to drop the four pounds she'd gained trying to show Kemp Hurley and Chris Plovert she wasn't some prissy girly girl who fussed over calories.

Even though she was.

After a short snooze and a steaming, lavender-scented face towel, Dylan threw the blanket off her palm frond green puff-sleeved Juicy hoodie and, out of pure boredom, reached for a stack of Merri-Lee's research materials. She scanned the headlines next to various photographs of Svetlana petting her thick side-braid: BLOND BOMBSHELL EXPLODES . . . BALL GIRL'S TEETH SOLD ON EBAY . . . NIKE SWOOSHES TO SVETLANA'S RESCUE WITH AN ENDORSEMENT DEAL . . .

Dylan flipped through dozens of pictures, then sighed hopelessly. Every one showed Svetlana in some bland white dress and athletic sneakers. Suhhh-noooozer!

"Mom, do you think there will be anyone my age at the spa who's *not* into tennis?"

"Cass!" Merri-Lee called back to her assistant, ignoring her daughter. "Are we confirmed on Svetlana's must-haves?"

Cassidy unbuckled her gold DG-stamped seat belt and appeared between Merri-Lee and Dylan on the brocade-carpeted aisle, her auburn curls pinch-clamped to the back of her head by a clear Scünci jaw clip.

"Spirulina detox smoothies, all the current tabloids with photos of Paris Hilton removed, thirty packs of chocolate mint Altoids, Tocca candles in lemon verbena, unscented baby wipes instead of toilet paper, and a gray kitty cat with haunting blue eyes." She tapped her pad with the tip of her pencil. "We're all set."

"Fan-tastic."

Cassidy turned on her ivory espadrille and wobbled back to her seat.

Suddenly, the plane dipped. It quickly recovered, but the sinking feeling in Dylan's stomach remained. Was she doomed to spend her spa vacation watching her mother kiss some blond Russian's ultra-toned butt? Gawd! Just because *she* wasn't famous or blond or toned or violent didn't mean she deserved to be ignored—did it?

"Aloha. We will now begin our initial descent into Honolulu," the pilot announced. "They had quite a thunderstorm last night, so everything will be beautiful and fresh for your arrival." His smooth voice sent an anxious ripple through Dylan's undefined abs.

Fresh!

It was time to make a fresh start.

No more comparing herself to Svetlana, or *anyone*. The next three weeks would be all about *Dylan* learning to love Dylan. No more super-skinny Westchester girls to compete with. No more alphas to obey. No more pretending to be someone she wasn't. No more crushing on boys who didn't crush back.

Her days of feeling inadequate were over!

And if anyone wanted to witness a real temper tantrum, all she had to do was stand in her way.

After dumping their LV luggage, slipping into matching floral-print sarongs, and nibbling on papaya slices from their complimentary exotic fruit basket, Dylan and Merri-Lee *click-clacked* down the palm-lined path to the resort's boutique. It was a Marvil tradition—no matter what city they were in, no matter how jet-lagged they were, they always made an effort to "go native."

The Kapalua shops were located in an open-air teak building overlooking a much-photographed black sand beach. As if infused with skin-softening emollients, a gardenia-scented breeze kissed their dry airplane arms. *Ahhhhhhh* . . . It made the private jet's cashmere blankets feel like loofahs in comparison.

Pre-shopping tingles ran down Dylan's pale spine as she stepped into the boutique's air-conditioned entryway.

"No!" she burped, stopping dead in her scarlet Louboutin slides and dropping her mom's birdlike arm. Light spilling from an elegant row of recessed fixtures glinted off the cream-and-silver fleur-de-lis wallpaper. Short, white, pleated tennis skirts hung next to white, sweat-absorbent polos. Against the far wall, Nikes, Adidas, New Balances, and Pumas were given the Jimmy Choo treatment. It was as though a group of

LBRs were sitting at the Pretty Committee's lunch table.

Where were Calvin and Chloé?

"This is supposed to be a high-end boutique, nawt a Lady Foot Locker," Dylan whisper-hissed to her mother.

Merri-Lee hitched her straw Gucci hobo higher on her shoulder. "When in Rome, Dylan. This is all state-of-the-art athletic wear." She gave her daughter a let's-make-the-most-of-it pat on the backside, then nudged her farther into the store. "Keep in mind," Merri-Lee said as she lifted a green raw-silk headband off a plastic display head and slipped it over her ponytail, "tennis skirts sit low on the waist and can be very flattering. And the ones with the built-in undies are just plain c-u-t-e. Meet at the dressing rooms in five?"

Dylan checked her silver Kenneth J. Lane watch. "Done."

She trudged over to the only rack that looked remotely acceptable. Just as she reached for a terry cloth cover-up with slight potential, Svetlana appeared on the plasma TV behind the register. On-screen, she gave her signature graphite tennis racket a quick peck and then lovingly stroked its strings as if they doubled as a harp.

"I love my Wilson. And you'll love watching me use it to serve up my A-game at this year's Aloha Open. See you there!" TV Svetlana winked, then tossed her blond braided hair-snake over her tanned shoulder—in slo-mo, of course.

Dylan giggled-smirked. Svetlana was obviously trying to work her way back into America's good graces. And it reeked of fake—like Massie's famous IT act, or Innocent Teacher act, where she loaded on the sweetness to avoid detention.

Just then, a perky Hawaiian salesgirl in tennis whites approached with I-work-on-commission enthusiasm. "Hi! I'm Ash! Can I take that for you?" She grabbed the terry cloth cover-up and flipped her dark, glossy hair over her shoulder.

"What's with the whiteout?" Dylan gestured 360 degrees to the Wonder Bread–colored clothes.

"Every year we clear out our designer inventory to make room for the Aloha collection. White's the official color of the Open, so everyone—players, guests, resort personnel"—Ash pinched her white Lacoste shorts—"wears it. It's big fun! I'll stick this in the dressing area for you and pull a few of our top sellers." She tilted her head and gave Dylan the once-over. "Size six, right?"

Dylan rolled her eyes in a how-dare-you sort of way. "Actually, it's a four."

Ash lifted her thick, doubting eyebrows. "Try this." She yanked a tiny pleated mini off the rack.

"Don't bother." Dylan waved away the skirt. "I'll pull my own things. I have very specific taste."

"Oh yeah?" Ash popped her collar. "How would you describe this *specific* taste of yours?" she challenged.

Good."

Ash gasp-turned to smile-greet a dangerously tanned man in madras golf slacks.

The instant she was alone, Dylan hung the size-four skirt back on the silver rack and grabbed the six.

In the back, outside the dressing room, Merri-Lee was

signing an autograph for a fiftysomething blonde who clearly did not have a best friend. If she did, this friend would have held a mirror up to the woman's wrinkled legs and stopped her from going out in nothing but a black one-piece and three-inch slides.

"I just luuuv your mother," the lady gushed in a husky voice. "Or is she your sister?"

She cracked up, the loose skin on her turkey neck shaking in time with her implants.

Merri-Lee joined in until the two were cackling like reunited sorority sisters. It didn't matter how many times some desperate fan busted out the old "Are you two sisters?" joke—Merri-Lee always lapped it up. Meanwhile, it left Dylan wondering if she looked like a forty-two-year-old woman.

Surrounded by white sportswear and mom jokes, Dylan wished she'd accepted Massie's invite to spend the summer in Southampton. What had made her think she would have any fun hanging out with her mother and a bunch of geriatric *Daily Grind* fans? Yes, they were in paradise. But paradise was only paradise if there was someone special to share it with.

Rolling her eyes, Dylan closed her dressing room door, tossed the white pleated skirt on the cold marble floor, and searched for her comfy terry cloth cover-up. But it had been replaced with a rack of blindingly white tennis outfits, tight racer-back tanks, and a row of Nike sneakers.

"Mom, I don't *do* white on white," Dylan whisper-yelled through the dressing room door.

"Excuse me for a moment, Helen," Merri-Lee said to her

stalker. "Dyl Pickles," she called, "everyone here wears tennis whites—it's tradition."

Dylan smacked the hanging clothes. "But I'm allergic to . . . *athletic*."

"Don't be ridiculous. Besides, I thought one of your summer goals was to drop four pounds."

Dylan's cheeks burned. Did the Polynesians need to know this?

"Try the Svetlana for Nike outfit," Merri-Lee insisted. "It's very forgiving."

Dylan sighed. It was pointless to argue. The AmEx black card was in her mother's Gucci, *not* hers, meaning she'd have to play by the rules. Besides, she planned on spending most of her time on the massage table, naked, sandwiched between Frette sheets and smothered in more oil than curly fries. And who knew? Maybe the Pretty Committee would bloat to size sixes and they could all dress up as tennis players next Halloween . . . either that or latte foam.

"Come out, Dee Dee. Let's see it." Her mom's puffy red lips appeared in the crack of the door. "Svetlana wore one just like it on the cover of *Sports Illustrated*." Dylan could hear Merri-Lee's thumbnails punch-tapping the keys on her Black-Berry. "I'm sure you look adorable."

"Whatevs," Dylan groaned, not bothering to check. She swung open the dressing room door and spun to give her mom the rear view. "White makes my butt look—"

"Hot," a male voice cut in.

Instinctively, Dylan shielded her barely covered rear

and inhaled sharply, preparing to unleash her wrath on the mysterious perv.

And then she saw *him*.

According to *Us Weekly*, Zac Efron was on a movie set filming yet another musical remake. But she was tempted to pluck one of this hawttie's honey-colored highlights for DNA testing, just to be sure.

"The fabric wicks sweat away before it even leaves your pores. See?" He hooked the elastic band of his own tennis whites, revealing a sliver of tanned, toned, rock-hard boy-belly.

Merri-Lee rested her perfectly manicured fingers on his shoulder. "Dylly, this is John Thomas Daley. His father owns this place."

"The store?" Dylan teased.

"The resort," Merri-Lee beamed.

"And the one next door," John added. He stuck out his hand to shake Dylan's.

"You can call me J.T. My dad goes by John."

"Is he as cute as you are?" Merri-Lee purred.

J.T. glanced down at his tanned knees and grinned.

Dylan rolled her eyes, silently apologizing to the HART (Hot Alpha Rich and Toned) for her embarrassing-times-ten mother.

The second Dylan gripped his warm boy-hand, she abandoned her whole only-crush-on-boys-who-are-going-to-crush-back summer goal. She was fully prepared to obsess over him.

"Aloha," she giggled shyly, hating herself for not pre-glossing.

"So"—J.T. turned to Merri-Lee—"is it true you're here to interview Svetlana Slootskyia?"

Gawd! Is a stint in rehab the only way to get noticed these days?

"Wow!" He blushed with awe as Merri-Lee nodded. "I mean, good luck with that. I heard she can be tough."

"I can handle it." Merri-Lee flexed her bicep.

Dylan turned away and clenched her fists.

"Did you know that *aloha* means 'hello' *and* 'goodbye'?" J.T. swiped his long, butterscotch-colored bangs to the side of his forehead.

"Dyyyylly." Merri-Lee nudged her daughter. "J.T. is talking to you."

"Huh?" Dylan asked, excusing herself from her I'm-invisible pity party.

"Did you know that aloha means 'hello' *and* 'goodbye'?" he asked again.

"Oh yeah. Totally." Dylan finger-combed her red curls, reinvigorated by his tidbit. She'd heard on *Animal Planet* that when a male is interested, he drops random scraps at the female's feet, something to do with the hunting instinct. Wasn't this aloha factoid the human version of that?

"Speaking of aloha, we're having a welcome dinner for the Open's VIPs tonight. You two should come."

"We were planning on it." Merri-Lee pulled the gold and white invite out of her Gucci and waved it like a victory flag. She was clearly offended J.T. hadn't *assumed* they were invited.

"You know, as *the* host of *The Daily Grind,* I *am* privy to—"

Her BlackBerry tooted the *Daily Grind* theme song. "I have to take this." She lifted her tissue-stuffed bags, and *poof,* Dylan's matchmaking mom was gone like Criss Angel.

Alone at last.

"Hey, J.T." Ash wave-walked over, her black high-pony swinging like a happy puppy's tail.

"Whaddup, Ash?" he mumbled, never taking his eyes off Dylan.

Ehmagawd, was he crushing back?

Perkyshorts got the hint and harrumphed to the front of the store.

"Those are pretty sweet kicks," he said, nodding at Dylan's shoes. He lifted one toned leg, revealing an identical shoe.

Dylan blew Merri-Lee a mental air kiss to thank her for picking the Nikes.

"So, are you the hard-core-into-tennis type?" He raised his brown brows. "Or the all-gear, no-idea type?"

"Puh-lease! I totally heart tennis," she lied. "I *have* to buy this outfit. I've already worn my other ones out."

He chuckled.

Did he think she was joking?

Lying?

Charming?

Fat?

"I think you should get that one." He smiled with his midnight blue eyes. "Come on, I'll walk you to the register."

Dylan thought about rescuing her sarong from the changing room but decided not to bother. Her new tennis persona wouldn't dream of wearing something that impractical and chic. Besides, the sweet smell of J.T.'s coconut-scented sunscreen had suddenly become something she couldn't live without, and it was now heading in the opposite direction.

"Oh no," she accidentally blurted as they reached a rack of white visors.

"What?" J.T. stopped walking and touched the small of her back.

"My mom has my AmEx black card in her purse."

J.T. grinned. "No worries. It's on me."

"Really?" Dylan beamed, and *not* because of the 100 percent discount.

"Really." He caught Ash's attention and air-scribbled. She nodded once. And just like that, they strolled out of the boutique without so much as stopping to pick up a complimentary mint.

"Love the outfit." Dylan smiled, the afternoon sun warming her air-conditioned shoulders. "My tennis elbow thanks you."

"You have tennis elbow?" he asked with grave concern.

Something in his expression made Dylan wonder if she had misused the term.

"Kidding," she tried.

His smile returned.

"You're funny."

"You're right," she giggled. "Thanks again for the dress."

"No problem. I'll have Ash send more up to your room." He

quickly scanned her. "Size six?"

"Four," she corrected him quickly.

"Four it is!" He waved once and turned toward the villas. "See you tonight."

"Yup. See ya tonight." Dylan rocked back on the rubber heels of her Nikes, hoping the boutique had a decent exchange policy.

"I feel like I'm in a floral-scented snow globe," Dylan whispered to Merri-Lee later that night.

They had just entered the massive tent on the hibiscus-lined bluff overlooking the twilit Pacific. Everywhere Dylan looked she saw white: white orchid centerpieces, white chandeliers dripping with pearls, white Mikasa china, frosted-white goblets, and, of course, white-clad tennis lovers sampling appetizers and predicting this year's Aloha Open champions. And it was all set to the driving electronic beats of the Chemical Brothers. An odd choice for a VIP dinner, but so were sneakers.

Feeling like a total mom-glom, Dylan quickly ditched Merri-Lee in search of someone worth texting home about.

She wove through the crowd in her silver Nike Zooms, her mom's diamond-studded four-leaf clover Chopard earrings swinging above the mesh straps of her Svetlana for Nike dress. In the absence of color and delicate fabrics, Dylan needed something that spoke to the side of her that wasn't selling out for a crush. Never had her lids been so smoky or her pulse points more saturated in ginger-blackberry DKNY Delicious Night perfume. Her red curls had been individually glossed, and one side was pinned above her ear. A full updo would have been too sophisticated for the sporty crowd, and all down would have eclipsed her fabulously high cheekbones. For someone who had spent the majority of her day on a dehydrating airplane and then been forbidden to wear black, Dylan looked pretty darn good.

"Excuse me, miss." A walking Abercrombie bag materialized in front of her, holding a silver tray. "Would you care for a prosciutto-wrapped melon ball in a soy and white wine reduction?"

"Given." Dylan stabbed some melon with a toothpick and lifted it to her mouth. A slab of prosciutto fell off the ball and landed on the yellow swoosh above the hem of her skirt. "Ooops." She flicked the oily scrap with her soy sauce–sticky fingers, leaving a dark streak on the porous material. "Why aren't you serving all-white food? Soy is white's worst enemy."

Abercrombie was just offering Dylan a napkin when she spotted J.T.

"Forget about it." She waved away the blond waiter, then hurried toward her idea of an Aloha Open trophy.

He was standing next to a giant ice sculpture of a tennis racket, shaking hands with a silver-haired couple and charming them with his dimple-flanked smile. He looked ah-dorable in his Lacoste polo and tuxedo tennis shorts, which was no easy feat.

"Awesome party," she blurted, then immediately regretted it. Massie always told her to act aloof around boys she liked.

"Hey, you." J.T. turned away from his geriatric audience

and focused his hotness on Dylan. His floppy brown hair was pokey with product, and his navy eyes made the Pacific backdrop seem unnecessary.

"That dress is a grand slam." He bent at the knee and mimed a forehand swing.

"Thanks!" Dylan scanned the crowed, trying to take in every detail of the night on which she was inevitably going to lose her lip-kiss virginity. But her brain must have been covered in Teflon, because nothing seemed to be sticking except J.T.'s hawtness.

"Follow me." He grabbed her wrist and led her to a nearby table. Getting pulled through the crowd by such a total HART made Dylan forget she was wearing an athletic dress. The way everyone was envy-staring, one would have thought she was draped in Lagerfeld.

J.T. lifted two flutes of sparkling white cider off a passing tray. Dylan accepted her mocktail graciously, then fake-sipped. Bubbly anything led to burping, and unfortunately, they weren't at that point in their relationship yet.

"So, do you surf?" Dylan consulted her mental list of "boy questions" as she strategically placed a white napkin on her soy stain.

"Nah. Tennis is way more exciting and far more demanding."

"Ah-greed." Dylan took another fake sip. "Do you play video games?"

"Tennis Wii is *awe*some. My friend Nick and I played for five hours last night. Get this—he actually sprained his finger trying to return my lob." His slammed his elbow on the silver tablecloth and rested his forehead in his hand. "I mean, who does that?"

"He must be in a lot of pain." Dylan pretended to care.

"Real pain is losing your Wii partner," J.T. sighed. "You play?"

Dylan shook her head no. The only Wii she was interested in was her and J.T.

A long moment of silence followed. Their eyes darted around the room—and then grazed over each other for a split second. J.T. rubbed his temple. Dylan finger-twisted her hair. She searched her mind for something to say, but nothing came. She felt trapped in an episode of *The Hills*.

All she wanted to do was burp, "Like me!" But she knew it was too soon. Instead, she pretended to be distracted by the popping bubbles in her champagne flute, as if they were sending her an urgent message that demanded her immediate attention.

Beyond the tent a soft breeze rustled the palm fronds, the surf ebbed and flowed against the black sand, wide-winged birds glided across the tie-dyed sky, and speedy little lizards scuttled past their feet. It was as if Mother Nature was working her magic all over the place, except when it came to her and J.T.

"So, what else are you into? You know, other than tennis?" Dylan asked, hoping for something she could respond to in earnest.

J.T. blinked as though he didn't quite understand the question. "Travel, I guess."

"Seriously? I *love* to travel. I traveled here all the way from Westchester, New York." She sat up a little taller.

"New York? No way!" He leaned closer. "Have you ever been to Ashe Stadium?"

"Come awn, *Ashe* me a hard one." She rolled her eyes, managing to avoid admitting she had no idea what that was.

"Okay." His eyes crackled with electricity. "Grass, clay, or hard?"

"Why choose one when you can have them all?" Dylan shrugged. Were those part of the spa package?

"Most people have a favorite surface—even Federer struggles on clay."

"Sucks to be h—" She paused. Was this person male or female? "Sucks to be Federer."

J.T. shook his head slowly from side to side, the corners of his red lips curled in a you're-quite-a-piece-of-work sort of way.

But a good piece of work or a bad piece of work? The uncertainty was making her palms itch.

"So, what's *your* favorite quality in a girl?" Dylan asked, hoping they still had a chance, even though they had different interests. After all, David Beckham hadn't picked Sporty Spice—he'd picked Posh. And who said lightning couldn't strike twice?

"Well, I can tell you what I *don't* like. My last girlfriend knew nothing about tennis. She was more into shopping," he practically spit.

Suh-nooozer!" Dylan blurted, surrendering to his dark blue eyes, even though shopping did seem like the best way to fight the jet lag that was tempting her to yawn in his face.

Just then, a warm breeze delivered a whiff of J.T.'s coconut-scented skin and rendered her powerless. So he was a little tennis-obsessed—she could pretend to be a size-four athlete for a week or two. How hard could it be?

"I mean, do you have any idea what it's like to talk to someone who goes on and on about something you have absolutely no interest in?" he asked, shaking his head.

"It sounds awful."

He looked her straight in the eye with an intensity that made her pits itch.

"My family has box seats for the Erickson-Sveningson match in three days. You should join us."

Dylan was tempted to Tom Cruise herself onto the chair and shout, "A *ten* just asked me out!" But she speed-nodded her acceptance instead.

A warm smile spread across J.T.'s chiseled face, and Dylan had a feeling she'd be burping in front of him by sunrise.

Suddenly, a collective gasp filled the tent. J.T.'s navy blue eyes drifted to the center of the crowd and held firm on the blonde standing beneath the pearl-coated chandelier.

Svetlana Slootskyia stood petting her signature French braid as if it were a charmed snake. Her sleeveless, sequin-covered tennis cocktail dress shimmered in the setting sun, boldly announcing that she wasn't going to hide from her scandal: in fact, she was going to shine. Her toned, tanned arms and long, slim legs more than justified her place on the cover of *Maxim*. But her narrow blue-green eyes and tight lips sent a clear message to her pervy boy-fans: "Don't even think about it."

As soon as everyone realized they were staring at Svetlana, the hum of voices, random bursts of laughter, and the clinking of silverware resumed immediately.

But J.T. didn't move. He didn't even blink.

Dylan swiveled, once again following his dreamy gaze to Svetlana "IntimidatinglyprettyinternationalstarNikeendorsed-*Maxim*covergirlWimbledonwinning" Slootskyia.

Reality hit Dylan like a barrage of high-speed tennis balls. When she'd met J.T. in the tennis shop, he hadn't been calling *her* hot—he'd meant her *dress* was hot. Specifically, her Svetlana for Nike dress.

If Svetlana was Tennis Barbie, Dylan was Raggedy Ew.

The party paparazzi and several Elph-wielding fans snapped away, and Svetlana smiled graciously for each and every one of them. She didn't look angry or dangerous, just poised and gracious as she pivoted to make sure everyone got what they came for.

But Dylan wasn't buying it. She had read enough *Us Weekly*'s to know that rehab doesn't work the first time.

All she had to do now was prove it.

"Cassidy, can you please do something about these waves?" Merri-Lee whipped off her headphones and tossed them onto the black director's chair. "They're killing my audio."

"Um . . ." The rattled assistant hurried to the edge of the precipice and searched the turquoise ocean for a possible solution.

Ever since the alarm beeped at 5 A.M., Merri-Lee had been a nervous wreck. Was her cream-colored pantsuit white enough? Was the sky blue enough? The breeze cool enough? Her blowout full enough? Were the interview questions edgy enough? Was the cliffside pagoda charming or tacky? Did the palm trees in the background look fake? Should Svetlana recline on the pink satin couch or sit? *Orrrrr* should they lose the couch altogether and go with something more sporty? Like a treadmill? Wait! Maybe they should forget the pagoda and move the shoot to the clay court. Or would it be better for Svetlana's new image to keep her in this Zen environment? What would Barbara do?

Dylan did what she could to reassure her mother over a pointless breakfast of hot lemon water and dry whole wheat toast points. But she had her own concerns and didn't really give it her all. True, this interview, if done right, would put Merri-

Lee in a whole new category of get-the-story telejournalists. But if Dylan could use this time to truly study Svetlana—her tennis style, her tennis lingo, her tennis elbow—she'd have a much better chance of convincing J.T. that she was just as worthy of his love as Svetlana. And in the big picture, that was much more important than this interview. After all, *The Daily Grind* featured high-profile celebs five days a week. But the chance to lose her lip virginity to a perfect ten would probably never happen again.

Dylan stepped into the pagoda. A maze of duct-taped camera wires had been stuck to the white wood floor by the crew, and Cassidy had seen to it that all of the star's needs had been met. A mini Sub-Zero fridge had been installed to keep the spirulina detox smoothies chilled, and a Paris Hilton–free stack of *Us Weekly*'s, *OK*'s, and *Hello*'s were fanned out on the teak coffee table. Thirty packs of chocolate mint Altoids were stacked into a pyramid beside the magazines, and the flames on the Tocca candles bowed in the island breeze.

"Pickles, have a seat on the couch for a minute," Merri-Lee said with an impatient smile. "We need a stand-in for Svetlana while we adjust the lighting."

Dylan sat immediately. How poetic! There she was trying to *be* Svetlana and she was asked to—

Re-owwwwwww!

A gray kitty cat with haunting blue eyes leaped up from underneath a throw pillow and pounced on top of the silver fridge. It hissed at her, baring its pointy, Gillette Venus–sharp teeth.

"What the—?"

"Thank you for getting me Boris." Svetlana extended her white bell sleeve–covered arms as she glided into the pagoda and lifted the kitty off the fridge. She held it against her Puma minidress and swayed back and forth. The silver S clips that held back her blond hair wink-reflected each time they caught the sun.

"Is he *yours*?" Dylan stood, more out of nervousness than respect.

"*Nyet.*" Svetlana shook her head no just in case Dylan didn't understand Russian. "*My* Boris is trapped in Moscow. Your president will not allow him to enter this country without quarantine. So I have Boris look-alikes until we are together again." She squat-pivoted next to the fridge and pulled out two green spirulina-soy lattes. "Have."

Unsure whether that was a question or a command, Dylan politely accepted.

"There's my little superstar," Merri-Lee gushed.

Dylan rolled her eyes. Her mother was constantly embarrassing her with silly nicknames and—

Merri-Lee pulled the tall blonde into a suffocating hug.

Oops. Wishful thinking.

"Mom-Coach sends these for you and delightful assistant Cassidy." Svetlana looked from Merri-Lee to Dylan and held out a red, heart-shaped tin containing black-caviar pierogi-and-cheese blintzes dipped in Valrhona chocolate.

Dylan almost choked on her green smoothie. "I am *nawt* her assistant—I'm her daughter."

"Really?" Svetlana studied them for a moment, then stroked Boris's tiny gray head. "You look like sisters."

"Did you hear that, Dylly? *Sisters!*" Merri-Lee lost herself in a fit of hysterics, her smile lingering long after the laughter faded.

On the outside, Dylan grinned with faux amusement. But on the inside, she imagined herself on the black beach below, tanning next to J.T. as the cobalt blue waves lapped against the shore. In this particular fantasy, he was feeding her BBQ Baked Lay's, admiring her curves, and begging her to tell him funny stories about the Pretty Committee. Oh, and she was *not* wearing white.

"Where *is* the charming Olga?" Merri-Lee glanced over Svetlana's shoulder.

"Mom-Coach could not be here. She is checking clay courts for dents."

"Well, thank her warmly for me." Merri-Lee quickly unloaded her nosh on a member of her lighting crew. "I'm so thrilled to have you here." She clapped as if she and Svetlana were off to their first Kappa Kappa Gamma social. "Please, have a seat."

Svetlana sat on the pink satin couch, knees firmly together. Dylan climbed up on the black director's chair just outside the pagoda and snapped her knees together too.

Knowing she had tons to learn if she wanted to turn the J.T. beach fantasy into a reality, Dylan switched her brand new LG Chocolate phone to camera mode. This way, she wouldn't miss a thing.

Her mother quickly briefed Svetlana on the nature of the interview, and complimented her on her beauty, poise, outfit, maturity, hair, business savvy, media savvy, and flawless skin. Then she ordered the makeup artist over for last-minute touch-ups. Once satisfied, Merri-Lee joined Svetlana and Boris on the couch.

"This is Merri-Lee Marvil coming to you from the Aloha Open in Kauai, Hawaii. I'm here with Wimbledon champ and cover model Svetlana Slootskyia. Welcome to *The Daily Grind*."

Svetlana smiled. "Thank you, Merri-Lee. It's very wonderful to be with you."

So far, Dylan had determined that the tan was real, the thick black eyelashes were fake, and the accent, even though it was gruff and hard to decipher, had a certain appeal.

"Svetlana, allow me to get to the heart of the matter. You went from big winner to sore loser. Care to comment?" Merri-Lee tilted her head to show how interested she was, her diamond tennis racket earring colliding with the side of her neck.

Svetlana stroked her thick blond snake-braid. "I will never be able to express how sorry I am for what I did to little Ali Chipley's teeth. But I bought her new ones, and they are much nicer than old ones, so Svetlana feels good about that."

Dylan snickered.

"Can you tell us what was going on in your head when you . . ."—Merri-Lee looked up, as if searching the thatched roof for the right words—". . . when you had the *episode*."

Svetlana chewed her tight bottom lip and held Boris to

her heart. "I have worked so hard and given up so much for tennis." She blinked back tears. "And when I lost that match, it felt like I had lost everything I had worked for. And not just me. My mom-coach, who gave up life to train me; my father, who worked three jobs to pay for lessons; and my brothers and sisters, who gave up time with comrades to visit my tournaments." She dabbed her blue-green eyes on Boris's fur.

Merri-Lee didn't say a word. It was one of her great interview techniques. Silence made her subjects so nervous and uncomfortable they ended up revealing more than they'd planned.

Dylan took a long, loud slurp of her smoothie. Svetlana seemed so fragile and vulnerable. But Merri-Lee held firm, nodding yes with gentle encouragement, silently communicating that they had all the time in the world.

"And," Svetlana sighed, "when I saw that ball girl congratulate my opponent, I felt like it was a slap. Not only to my cheek, but the cheek of my family. And I went into a *blond* rage."

Dylan snickered again. Had Svetlana brilliantly coined a new term, or was her English worse than her temper? Either way, it was awesome.

"And what went through your mind?" Merri-Lee crossed, then uncrossed her pale legs.

"I'm afraid I cannot recall." Svetlana gazed out at the horizon.

Merri-Lee gave Svetlana's hand a comforting pat, then turned to face the flat screen on the coffee table.

"Maybe it will help you remember if we take a look at it."

Svetlana's blue eyes widened as the screen came to life. In slo-mo and set to "Apologize" by Timbaland featuring OneRepublic, the video showed roses raining down on the court as perky Bessie Evans blew air kisses at her fans. Ali Chipley threw a handful of balls in the air like a giddy graduate and ran-bounced with open arms to congratulate her. Just before Ali and Bessie made contact, Svetlana pulled back her racket like a Spalding bat and swung straight at Ali's face. Little white teeth shards flew from her mouth like Tic Tacs.

"Make it stop!" Svetlana cried, waving away the horror.

Merri-Lee slit her throat with her index finger, letting Cassidy know it was time to cut the feed. "Bring back any memories?" she asked sweetly.

"No." Svetlana shook her head in shame.

Merri-Lee leaned in closer, her lips pursed dramatically as she waited for a better answer.

"I will never forgive myself," Svetlana said slowly, lowering her gold-dusted eyelids.

Merri-Lee addressed the camera. "Along with veneers, Ali Chipley received one-point-three million dollars, box seats to Wimbledon for life, and a spot on a new reality show called *Celebrity Survivors,* along with Naomi Campbell's assistant."

Suddenly beaming with renewed pride, Svetlana nodded as if all of this somehow absolved her.

Dylan ran her tongue over her BriteSmile and wondered if she should be trying to emulate someone who knocked out a ball girl's teeth. And then she thought of J.T. and had her answer. Besides, it wasn't like Svetlana woke up that morning determined to hurt Ali. She just snapped, as would any tightly wound athlete who'd given up her life for no reason.

Merri-Lee patted her perfect blowout, then turned to face her subject. "Svetlana, do you think you are rehabilitated?"

"Yes. I have watched sun set on my anger."

Merri-Lee knit her thin brows.

"It is truth." She let Boris lick her wrist. "We did several activities at the center I never had time for as child. Some-ores and campfires and hikes. I made girlfriends and had gentle pillow fights." Svetlana's lids fluttered with emotion. "I tapped into part of Svetlana I never got to explore. Of course, if I could take back what I did, I would. But in a way, I am glad it happened. I lost my temper but found real me."

Dylan felt her throat tighten. No wonder Svetlana had snapped. Without the weekly overnights at Massie's, where the Pretty Committee gossiped about their crushes, complained about teachers, and made fun of LBRs, Dylan would have become a raging tennis beast, too. Well, minus the tennis part.

"But it wasn't all fun. It was hard work, too—daily therapy sessions and hours of meditation. I've incorporated Zen into my everyday routine. It has been life changing." Svetlana crossed her legs, demonstrating the "om" position.

Trying to cross her legs Svetlana-Zen style, Dylan noticed a green splotch on her box-pleated skirt. How had that gotten there? Noting Svetlana's spotless LWTD (Little White Tennis Dress), Dylan wondered, *How does she keep her whites so white?*

Merri-Lee took a deep breath. "Well, Svetlana, I have to

say it's been an absolute pleasure to speak with you. You are a remarkable young lady, and I think we can all learn something from you. I know at least this fan"—Merri-Lee pointed to herself—"will be cheering you on out there."

"Thank *you* and all people out there who have given me and Slootskyia family a second chance. Before, I just do it all for me. This time," she sniffled, "I just do it for you." She smiled like a seasoned spokesmodel and looked directly into the camera. "Nike: Just Do It."

Dylan rolled her eyes. She felt like she was watching a sappy *Lifetime* movie—ads and all.

Curling her collagen-enhanced lips into a dazzling smile, the host addressed her public. "This is Merri-Lee Marvil for *The Daily Grind,* coming to you from the Aloha Open. And remember, if you're not watching, you're not living." She held her smile for the requisite seven seconds, then whipped the mike off her white Ralph Lauren Polo dress.

"That's a wrap, guys." She stood. "That was Emmy-worthy, Svetlana. Nice job. Now, if you'll excuse me, I'd like to get this off to my editor aysap."

"Of course. Thank you for your time." Svetlana kissed Boris and waved goodbye. "Enjoy the nosh."

The rest of the crew members offered Svetlana sympathetic grins as they scurried about dismantling the set. Ignoring them, she began making her way across the grassy lawn toward the bungalows.

"What an interview!" Dylan yelled, grabbing her LG and chasing Svetlana across the grassy lawn.

"Thank you." Svetlana stopped and dumped an entire box of chocolate mint Altoids in her mouth, then handed Dylan the empty metal tin.

She gripped it hard, hoping some of Svetlana's DNA would seep into her pores.

"Mmmmmm." Svetlana chewed, then blew her chocolate mint breath straight up Boris's tiny black nostrils. "Russia Boris loved this."

American Boris sneezed.

"Question." Dylan eagerly set her phone to record. "How did you get your braid so tight? I always have little pieces that poke out, but yours is so smooth and even." She reached out to pet it. "Is it hair spray? Mousse? Extensions? Or a combo of all three?

Just as Dylan's hand was about to make contact, the tennis phenom grabbed her wrist and twisted it back down to her side. The pain was so severe Dylan dropped her phone and yelped.

"Ehmagawd—ouch!"

"Camera's off, interview's over!" Svetlana barked. Boris hissed.

"Woah—the devil wears Puma!" Dylan took a step back and rubbed her wrist. "What about everything you said about Zen and meditation and being sorry?"

Svetlana stared at Dylan's mouth.

"What?" Dylan felt her cheeks burn.

"Are those teeth real?"

Dylan took a step back, her heels sinking in the spongy grass. "Of course they are."

Svetlana swung an imaginary racket toward Dylan's glossy mouth.

"What are you *doing*?" Dylan's ears buzzed with fear.

"Why do you think you are worthy to touch Svetlana?" The tennis star cracked her hair-snake like a whip. "You are just loserfan, too sloppy to be an athlete and—"

"I am *nawt* a fan!" Dylan shouted, her forehead starting to bead with sweat as the midmorning sun warmed the lush resort.

"Correction." Svetlana leaned forward until they were practically button nose to button nose. "You are a loserfan *stalker*!"

Then she head-butted Dylan.

"Ow! My skull!" Dylan grabbed her head, hearing a landline ringing inside her brain. "I think you gave me a concussion!" She whipped the empty Altoids tin at Svetlana, but accidentally hit Boris in the back left paw.

Without looking back, she scooped up her LG, put one silver Nike in front of the other, and ran as if her teeth depended on it.

"Ah-*lo*-ha!" Dylan burped that afternoon, the heavy bamboo door of the meditation room slamming shut behind her.

Reee-owwww! Boris meowed from somewhere inside in the dimly lit chamber. Svetlana's jaw clenched.

She was sitting alone, legs crossed, in the center of a caramel sand–covered floor with her eyes closed. Rake marks and tiny paw prints swirled around her. The pink travertine walls oozed water, which trickled into a gardenia-filled pond that flowed along the edges of the room. Birds chirped, waves lapped, and a deep man's voice chanted, "Ommmmm," over and over again, thanks to the sound effects that were piped into the candlelit chamber.

"Can we talk?" Dylan stomped over to Svetlana, leaving a Nike footprint trail in the sand.

"*Nyet.*" Svetlana's eyelids fluttered. She looked almost angelic in a white satin robe with her blond hair-snake wrapped around her head like a halo.

"Wrong answer." Dylan stomped. A cloud of sand puffed around her yellow pom-pom tennis socks.

Svetlana's eyes snapped open. "Back for seconds?" She reached out and pinched Dylan's calf.

"Owie!" Dylan yelped. Her skin prickled with fear and

adrenaline. No way was she going to endure another head butt. She backed up a few sand-print steps in case she needed to make another run for it. "You're totally insane—I can't believe you almost fooled everyone with your whole *transformation* act."

"What you mean *almost*?" Svetlana smirked. "Everybody adores Svetlana again thanks to your mom-host."

Dylan pursed her Nars Peachy Keen–smeared lips. "Puhlease! You practically twisted my arm into the Nike swoosh."

"So what?" Svetlana unraveled her braid-snake from its halo. "No one saw it, and no one will believe what a little red pimple like you has to say."

Dylan pinched her hips with renewed hope. "Wait, you think I'm *little*?"

"Just the brain." Svetlana stood, brushing sand off her slippery-smooth robe.

"Oh yeah? Then how do you explain *this*?" Dylan waved her LG.

"It's called phone, Pimple." Svetlana knocked it to the sand. "Now go. I must get back to meditation."

"Not until I watch your little outburst under the candlelight." Dylan held up the phone and thumbed through the buttons. Her hands shook, knowing they could get smacked or snapped at any given moment. "I want to hear the part where you called me a sloppy loserfan again. The acoustics in here are great and I—"

What?" Svetlana released her honey-colored braid and clenched her fists.

"I wonder what the International Tennis Association will say when it sees you've fallen off the temper-tantrum wagon?" Dylan positioned her LG under Svetlana's narrow blue-green eyes. A shot of the post-interview arm-twist was frozen on screen. "This little thing is amazing. It's limited edition—Merri-Lee got it in her Oscar swag bag. It stores hours of video."

"How did you—"

"Just before you knocked the phone out of my hand I pressed record." Dylan winked. "Not bad for a *little* brain, huh?" Her heart thumped as Svetlana's smug expression darkened like the Hawaiian sky moments before a tropical storm.

"Thanks to your backhand, it was lying in the grass, so I have a few nice shots of your frilly underwear and—"

"Give to me." Svetlana swiped her claws Boris style as Dylan dropped the phone down the V of her lemon-yellow Fila minidress and folded her arms across her chest.

"After Nike sees this, the only thing you'll be endorsing is kitty litter," Dylan announced.

"How do I know you're not bluffing?" Svetlana's eyes flashed as she tightened the satin tie on her robe.

A new CD track blasted a series of loud, deep "ommm's" through the room.

Dylan reached inside her dress and pressed play on her LG.

Why do you think you are worthy to touch Svetlana? You are just loserfan, too sloppy to be an athlete and—"

"I am nawt a fan!"

"Correction. You are a loserfan stalker!"

"Ouch! My skull! I think you just gave me a concussion."

Dylan hit pause. Svetlana grinded her teeth, her dewy pink cheeks purple with rage. She muttered something in Russian that sounded a lot like "spit on your neck."

"Should I rewind to the part where you twisted my arm?"

"Enough," Svetlana demanded, clawing at Dylan's built-in sports bra, trying to swipe the phone.

Dylan jumped back, sending granules of sand skittering around her ankles. "Did you know I can zap this clip to *The Daily Grind* with the push of a button? Isn't that incredible?"

"You would not dare." Svetlana sneered, lunging once again at Dylan's chest.

Dylan pulled out her LG and mimed pressing SEND. "Or maybe Nike would like to see it?"

"Noooo!" Svetlana bent down and whipped a votive against the pink travertine. Glass shattered everywhere, hot wax splattered across the wall, and something landed on Dylan's head with a *thwack*. Sharp objects began ripping into her scalp.

"Ehmagawd, I've been hit!" she shrieked, then reached for her head, expecting to find a tangle of glass shards, red hair, and gooey brain-blood. But instead, she slammed into a four-pound ball of kitten fur.

"Ahhhhhhh!" Dylan frantically tried to swat Boris off her head.

"Reeee-owwww!" The cat dive-bombed into the sand and

scurried for the nearest corner, hissing as his paw landed in a puddle of molten wax.

Svetlana was breathing heavily. "You will not do this to me," she screamed, whipping another votive at the wall. Then another. And another.

Dylan simply stepped aside, pulled her phone out, and began recording it all. She couldn't have planned this better if she'd tried.

After the last candle had been tossed, Svetlana dropped to her knees and ran her fingers through the sand, whisper-counting in Russian. Several calming breaths later, she stood up again and smoothed her white skirt.

"What you want from me? An apology? Because Svetlana really didn't mean to—"

"I want a lot more than an apology." Dylan tucked the phone back into the V of her dress.

"Anything." Svetlana pulled each one of her long, slender fingers until it cracked.

Dylan put her hand on the bamboo door, just in case she needed to make a run for it, and then blurted, "Teachmeeverythingyouknowabouttennis."

"You want . . . tennis lessons?" Svetlana's flawless forehead crinkled.

Dylan nodded yes. "Times ten. I want to *become* the game."

You?" She rolled her blue-green eyes. "Mission impossible."

Dylan made a move for her phone.

"Okay, wait! Svetlana is just joking." A tight smile cut

across her face. It looked like she had poo cramps. "If you could please share why you hunger for such knowledge."

"Nawt that it's any of your business"—Dylan twirled a strand of glossy red hair around her finger—"but it has to do with getting a certain crush to crush back."

"You do this for a *boy*?" Svetlana flared her nostrils. "How pathetic."

"Puh-lease! You've given up your entire life for a *sport*. How is *that* any less pathetic?"

Svetlana opened her tight-lipped mouth to respond, but nothing came out.

Fifteen-love, Dylan.

Finally, she swallowed hard. "How many lessons must I give?"

"Until J.T. likes me back—"

"J.T.?" Svetlana threw back her head and laughed.

"You know him?" Dylan's cheeks burned.

"*Nyet.*" Svetlana quickly sobered. "But you Americans have such silly names."

Dylan crossed her arms. "Um, your nickname is *Sweat*."

"And yours is Pimple Loserfan!" Svetlana air-popped an imaginary zit.

Dylan held up her phone and let the unspoken threat hang in the gardenia-scented air.

"Okay, okay." Svetlana waved her palms in defeat. "I will help."

"Good. I'll be at your bungalow in two hours. Make sure

your hairstylist is there, and pull out some of your cute dresses. I'm running low."

Svetlana cocked her head. "Size six?"

"Four!" Dylan slammed the bamboo door behind her and hurried to the poolside café.

This LG Chocolate blackmailing was making her hungry.

"Love it!" Dylan burped.

She had spent the last four hours in Svetlana's bunga-low, staring at her reflection while Ingrid, Svetlana's busty personal stylist, wove extensions in her hair before perma-straightening it with chemicals that smelled like cabbage. When Ingrid left to ice her aching wrists, Dylan admire-stroked her twelve-inch, serpentine side-braid, wondering if J.T. would notice her striking resemblance to the Little Mermaid.

"Ariellllll," Dylan burped again.

Boris opened his haunting blue eyes, yawned, then curled back into his sleep-ball on the dirty-clothes pile in the middle of the room.

"Why must you belch words like a man?" Svetlana hit pause on the remote and sat up on her white (of course!) satin–covered bed. An image of herself midserve was frozen on the giant flat screen across from her.

Dylan considered answering but decided not to bother. How could she explain humor to a girl who chased balls across hot clay courts for *fun*? Instead, she crossed "Get hair like Svetlana" off her list and moved on.

"Now show me how to get that ah-dorable braid-swing

you get when you're hitting a ball." Dylan grabbed Svetlana's boar-bristle paddle brush off the mirrored vanity. She swung her arm back, then whacked it through the humid air.

But her new braid hung limp. Nothing could swing in this heat. "Any chance of putting the AC on in here?"

"*Nyet.*" Svetlana stood up and padded across the moist marble floor to jack up the thermostat even more. "Humidity keeps muscles limber. Get used to it. If you want to be world-class athlete, you have to suffer."

Dylan thumb-typed "extreme heat" into her LG as Svetlana looked on.

The mere sight of the device clearly put Svetlana on edge. She crossed the room and climbed the two limestone steps that led to the frosted glass spa-Jacuzzi nestled in the corner by the French doors. The glass doors opened to a lush garden, which was now drenched in the light of the pink Hawaiian sunset. Standing next to the tub, Svetlana powered on the jets, which burst to life with a frothing grumble.

"Where is my Epsom salt? WHO TOOK MY EPSOM SALT?" Her callused heel smashed up against the off button. The tub water rippled before going flat.

"Tem-puur." Dylan waved her phone at Svetlana from across the room. "Anyway, forget the bath—we still have wardrobe and tennis lingo and diet to cover before bed."

Svetlana spun around and hurried through the open French doors behind her. "Ugh!" She grabbed a handful of pink plumeria blossoms off a budding tree and crushed them between her fists. Mangled petals slipped through her quaking fingers as she paced the patio, mumbling in Russian.

"Hey, Svet," Dylan called from the safety of a white satin ottoman at the foot of the bed, "did you say your designer was in the suite next door?"

"I have idea." Svetlana turned, her rehearsed media smile hard at work. "Why don't we just go out to court and volley?"

Dylan grinned. It was nice to see her embracing their partnership. "Is there a mirror out there?"

"*Nyet.*" Svetlana unzipped her white Nike warm-up jacket and fanned her reddening cheeks.

"Well, how am I going to see how I look swinging and playing if I don't have a mirror?"

"Dee-lann, this is silly waste of time." Svetlana marched over to the ottoman and peered down at Dylan's newly straightened hair.

"No, it's not." Dylan stood. "I saw the way J.T. looked at you. I want *that*." Her voice trembled, struggling to support the weight of her words: words heavy with humiliation and frustration and LBR potential.

Because seriously! How pathetic was this whole blackmail scheme?

Most normal girls would down a dozen Entenmann's cookies and come to terms with the fact that their crush was already crushing on an international tennis star. And they'd move on. But Dylan refused to give up that easily. Those days were over. She was tired of stepping aside. Tired of the spotlight passing by on its search for someone better to illuminate, like Massie or her mother or Svetlana. For once, *she* wanted to shine. And not because she craved attention, but because she wanted to know that someone special truly believed she belonged there.

Someone other than herself.

"He was looking at *me*?" Svetlana's smile softened. With an extra spring in her stride, she bounced toward the mirror-covered door that connected her suite to the adjacent one.

Who?" Dylan followed the leggy blonde, her stomach sinking when she realized what she'd just revealed.

"This J.T. you are talking about—he looked at Svetlana in certain way?" Her blue-green eyes widened, making her look her real age of fifteen, as opposed to her rage-age of twenty-five.

Dylan tugged her hair-snake and waved away Svetlana's question. "So not the point. Now, let's talk outfits." The last thing she needed was to make Svetlana aware of J.T.'s irresistible hawtness. Because if she liked him and he knew it, Dylan would be playing singles for the rest of the summer.

"Fine. Now, enter." Svetlana held open the door and waved Dylan through.

The connecting suite was just as humid, but there was no canopy bed, spa-Jacuzzi, or fireside sitting area. Instead, bolts of varying shades of white, sweat-resistant fabrics were stacked along the walls like contestant finalists, all vying for the chance to become Svetlana's next tournament fashion statement. Eight rows of tennis shoes covered the marble floor, each one sprinkled with mentholated Gold Bond foot powder, ready for battle. And a gallery of plastic Svetlana look-alikes—each frozen in a different action pose—donned custom-made outfits. There was a new one for each of the tournament's seven rounds.

The suite was a seven-thousand-dollars-a-night walk-in closet.

"Ehmagawd, these are ah-mazing!" Dylan said, fingering the rice paper–thin fabric of a backless shift dress.

Svetlana brushed past her and stopped in front of the second mannequin, which was wearing a ribbed tank with a built-in navy ribbon belt and tulip-shaped skirt. "Does *amazing* mean *awful* in your country? If it *does*, then, yes, you are right. It is *amazing*." She yanked the ribbon out of the top and cracked it Catwoman style. "Winsome, what did I tell you about colors?"

A petite twentysomething in an orange tank dress emerged from behind a mountain of fabric. Dozens of pins pierced the rubber toes on her lime green Chucks, as if she were some sort of voodoo doll. Winsome was the first person Dylan had seen in two days who wasn't wearing white. She felt like Dorothy landing in Oz.

"Hi, I'm Svetlana's designer." She even had a high-pitched munchkin voice that complimented her shock of platinum Gwen Stefani–meets–Marie Antoinette hairdo.

"I'm Dylan. I luhv your—"

"And what is this?" Svetlana gut-punched a mannequin wearing short shorts and a glitter-covered sports bra. "Where is the belly chain?"

Winsome quickly caught the dummy before it toppled over. "Cartier is sending it over this aft—"

"And *this*?" Svetlana bared her fangs at a hippie-chic eyelet dress. "I asked for *eyelet*!"

"That *is* eyelet." Dylan had to correct her with an eye roll.

"No, *this* is eyelet." Svetlana picked up a black Sharpie and scribbled bold flowers all over the pretty white mini.

"Svetlana, those are *rosettes*," Winsome said evenly.

"Maybe in *your* country!" Svetlana wrote NYET across the dress and slammed down the marker.

"Svetlana, stop! These are cute times ten!"

Winsome shot Dylan a grateful smile.

Svetlana towered over the designer, her blond braid resting on the girl's bare shoulder. "I said I wanted the skirt shorter," she hissed.

"Right. You did. And you're right." Winsome pulled a pin out of her shoe and speed-fastened the hem an inch higher.

"So, Svetlana, tell Winsome why we're here." Dylan tapped the screen of her LG with a French-manicured nail tip.

"Tennis clothes," Svetlana managed. "Anything she wants."

"Of course!" Winsome finished the hem and then reached for her sketch pad, pulling a charcoal slab out of her platinum updo.

Their words washed over Dylan like the spa's luxurious Vichy shower. Was this how alphas were treated *all* the time?

"Sooo, what's the fantasy?" Winsome hopped up on a tall

sealed box marked WORN ONCE. DESTROY. She knocked the heels of her custom-made platform Chucks against the cardboard with glee. "I can do anything but beading. My fingers are too plump for detail work. Luckily, there's a woman on the mainland with baby hands. She's old but fast."

"I don't need beads." Dylan sat down next to Winsome. She peered over the designer's bony shoulder at the fresh page in her sketchbook, hoping it might be the last white thing she ever saw. "I want color. Lots of color. Ella Moss meets Puma with vertical stripes. They are slimming, don'tcha think?"

"Ab-so-luuuut-leeee!" Winsome narrowed her eyes and began sketching like a girl possessed.

"Arrrrrrrrrrr," Svetlana yawned with her entire face. She was standing among the mannequins, looking just as bored as they did.

"This heat is making me thirsty," Dylan said to Svetlana, loving the power this little blackmail scam was giving her. "I'd like a mango smoothie. Winsome?"

The designer immediately put down her sketch pad and stood up. "What can I get you?"

Dylan shook her head no. "*We* should keep working."

Winsome knit her platinum eyebrows in confusion.

"Svetlana will get them." Dylan stroked her red braid with the confidence and composure of a mob boss.

"I am no waitress!" Svetlana smacked one of the mannequins on the neck.

Dylan walked over to Svetlana. "Not yet. But you will be when I destroy your career," she whisper-hissed. This constant battle was trying her patience. Why couldn't Svetlana accept her role as a slave and just go with it?

Winsome glanced from her boss to Dylan back to her boss, as if she were watching a heated match in a game she barely understood.

Svetlana stepped away from the dummy. "Fine, what would you like?" she growled through clenched teeth.

Thirty-love, Dylan!

"Um, whatever she's having?" Winsome said like she was asking a question.

Svetlana spun on her Nikes, her blond braid slicing the humid air and slap-landing against her bare back.

"And don't bother spitting in it, 'cause you're taking the first sip," Dylan called after her.

As soon as Svetlana slammed the French doors behind her, Winsome turned to stare at Dylan in awe. "That was epic. She never listens to *anyone*. See this scar?" She pointed to a raised line above her brow. "I designed a Grecian dress that made her look like a goddess. I told her she looked beautiful, and she threw her championship ring at my eye."

Dylan leaned into get a better look at the damage. "How come?"

"She can't take compliments. She *hates* them. They make her violent." Winsome charcoal-drew a sad emoticon on her bare knee, then quickly smudged it away.

Dylan raised her eyebrows. "Why stay? You could design for anyone!"

"She's a walking ad for me." Winsome shrugged. "And if I

want to start my own label one day, I need to . . ." Her voice trailed off. "You know, you're the first friend she's ever had on tour."

"Really?" Dylan wanted to point out that she was hardly a friend, but suddenly she felt an odd tug of sympathy for Svetlana.

Winsome grabbed a bolt of purple and yellow Pucci-esque fabric from the discarded-color pile in the far corner of the suite. "Now, let's make you even more gorgeous than you already are!" She charged toward Dylan with vigor, but stopped short. "Wait. You don't mind if I call you gorgeous, do you?" She shielded her face with the fabric, just in case.

"Not even a little bit." Dylan beamed.

Diiiing-donnnng!

The following morning, Dylan tightened the bow on her sunset orange silk Tocca for Kapalua Spa robe and padded across her and Merri-Lee's bungalow. Her belly rumbled, knowing that the Salty Surfer Breakfast for two was waiting for her under a steamy silver dome on the room service cart. She was meeting Svetlana on her private court in an hour for their first practice, and she wanted to be well fueled for the workout.

"Alo-ha!" she blurted as she opened the door.

But a stack of boxes, not pancakes, stared back. A note on the cardboard, charcoal-written in happy loops, read:

For Dylan Marvil:
The most Marvil-ous muse ever. ☺
XOX Winsome

"Yayyy!" Dylan tossed her long red side-braid over her shoulder, then dragged the boxes inside. Starting the morning with a compliment and new clothes beat a hearty breakfast any day. Was this how Massie felt *every* time she got her daily delivery of Glossip Girl? And if so, no wonder she always walked around with a today-is-my-birthday attitude.

Diving into one of the shoe-size boxes first, Dylan pulled out a pair of lavender heart–covered platform sneakers named Forty-Love. The second pair was pewter mesh covered with metallic-red letters that spelled out MARVIL-OUS. A third pair was light green satin with a brown leather toe. Winsome had named them Mint Chocolate Chip, after her and Dylan's mutual love for the ice cream flavor.

For every shoe there was a matching outfit. A light lavender V-neck striped hooded dress. A red romper with tiny gray pinstripes. A green argyle vest with a tartan mini, intended to be worn over brown boy shorts.

Little Dylan-esque touches took each piece from adorable to utterly enviable: gray socks with peacock feathers instead of pom-poms, colorful satin headbands-turned-sweat-wickers, silver M FOR MARVIL-OUS hair pins, and a ruby red Swarovski tennis bracelet made to match her new, sparkling, custom-made red rhinestone racket! There was even a box of metallic gold tennis balls monogrammed with Dylan's initials in green.

The only thing missing was *white*.

If only her mother had been there to witness this bounty. Maybe then she'd realize how important her daughter really was. But she had been behind closed doors on a teleconference call with her producers since seven o'clock and had given Dylan strict instructions not to disturb her. Dylan sighed. She hoped, at least, that the intentional smattering of boxes and Svetlana-embossed tissue wrap would tip her mom off when she emerged.

"Now, what to wear?" Dylan scanned the volcano of clothes, wondering what would capture J.T.'s attention the fastest. She decided on a Diane von Furstenberg–inspired V-neck wrap dress with yellow, blue, and green Missoni-ish zigzags. Once she paired the dress with M.A.C. Copper Sparkle eye shadow and sweatproof YSL mascara, Dylan knew she'd look tennis hawt and then some.

Forgetting all about the Salty Surfer Breakfast, she slid on her Mint Chocolate Chips and left the bungalow with red-carpet confidence. It was time for her first lesson.

As usual, the sky was deep blue and cloudless. The tropical flowers opened their vibrant petals for the buzzing bees and hummingbirds. And the soft onshore breezes carved row after row of smooth waves that reminded Dylan of a plus-size pair of sapphire-colored corduroys.

On the lush, flower-flanked stone path that led to the public courts, Dylan bounced past two spa attendants in matching whites and old-school Ray-Bans. They lowered their black glasses when she passed.

"Want me much?" she giggle-mumbled under her breath.

Securing her Dior wraparound sunglasses, Dylan pretended not to notice the multitude of double takes she got as she sauntered across the grounds. Blissfully, she inhaled the fragrant island air and exhaled everything else. She would not be overlooked anymore.

At the courts, she spotted J.T. leaning against a gleaming chain-link fence, dabbing sweat off his brow with a gray wristband. Then he shook hands with a cute college-age boy whose pit sweat–flooded Fila shirt seemed to say, "I ran my butt off and lost."

Swinging her rhinestone-covered racket, Dylan mind-sang lyrics to J.T.'s (the famous one) "This Can't Just Be Summer Love" and timed her saunter to the groove-steady beat. As she neared the tennis greens, she saw Aloha Open banners and Nike swooshes adorning the courts and their aluminum pull-down seats. But nothing was more captivating than J.T. (the hawt one) and his caramel-colored highlights. His bangs were side-swept across his forehead, the tips kissing his black lashes and surrounding his navy eyes like a tiger-striped picture frame.

"Hey, Dylan!" he shout-waved.

Dylan's stomach lurched like one of those tennis ball–spitting machines. Her name coming from his mouth sounded eerie. Like when something you dream about actually comes true.

"Cool braid," he called.

Dylan grabbed her faux hair with faux surprise, as if spending four hours extending and straightening it with a busty woman named Ingrid was so normal she forgot others might find it something to behold.

"Oh, hey," she said, injecting her tone with just the right amount of never-expected-to-find-*you*-here.

"Are you playing today?" J.T. misted his rosy cheeks with Evian.

"Given," Dylan said with plenty of *duh*!

"Wanna volley?" he said, his eyes on her red crystal–covered racket.

"Um . . ." What did *volley* mean again? Dylan looked over at the courts and saw a group of seven-year-olds working on their serves. The serious players—the ones competing in the Aloha Open—practiced on private courts to avoid being studied by the competition.

"Is that a *yes*?" He placed a warm hand on her shoulder, putting her sweatproof fabric to the test.

"I'd love to, but, um, I'm playing Svetlana today."

"Wait. You're *friends* with Svetlana?" His eyes widened and he gripped the chain-link fence.

"Totally."

Behind him, the Pacific Ocean glinted in the sunlight.

"And you play together?"

Dylan nodded yes, as if this were something everyone wearing white had known for years.

"Wow. You must be . . . Wow . . . Do you think I could . . . Wow. I mean, could I just watch you guys warm up or something?" His voice cracked a little as he ran a hand through his adorably sweaty bangs.

"Oh, I'd love that," Dylan lied to his hopeful smile.

Was he more obsessed with tennis or Svetlana?

Not that it mattered. He was the kind of guy best friends fought over.

Dylan clutched her custom racket for strength. "Well, actually, Svetlana's feeling a little sensitive about her serve today. And it may be better if we just, you know—"

"Sure. Of course. I get it." He waved the thought away like a smelly jockstrap. "But we're still on for the Brady Erickson match tomorrow, right?"

Yes! Maybe he did like her after all.

But just in case, Dylan thought it best to end this before the sexy sports-model and her latest pleated mini came searching for her tardy pupil and proved Dylan wrong.

"Yup, see you at the match."

"Oh, and um, one more thing," he stammered to his Adidas.

OMG! Was he going to ask for her phone number? The name of her favorite flower? Her hand in marriage?

She casually wiped her clammy hands on her braid.

"Yes," Dylan said sweetly, hoping to fill him with the confidence he needed to finish his question.

"Do you think you could . . ." He scratched his head and squinted against the bright sunlight.

"Yes?" Dylan took an encouraging half-step forward. He still smelled like coconuts. "What is it?"

"Do you think you could, um, wear something a little more"—he swallowed—*"white?"*

Dylan's insides gasped and her outsides blushed. "You didn't seriously think I'd wear *this*, did you?" she managed. But she looked so hawt!

He shrugged, looking slightly embarrassed.

"Puh-lease!" Dylan hate-gripped her red Swarovski crystal–covered racket.

"It's not me, it's my dad. He's so old school," J.T. insisted. "Personally, I *like* your dress."

"You do?" Dylan's cheeks faded back to their natural pale state. "What about my racket?" She tilted it so the crystals caught the sun. They cast flecks of light on the thick green grass beneath their feet.

"Love it!" He grinned.

Love you, Dylan wanted to shout. But instead she said a quick goodbye and bounced off to Private Court One, where Svetlana was probably pace-waiting for her.

"You are three-and-one-half-minutes late." Svetlana tossed a fuzzy yellow ball in the air and slammed it onto the red clay court with her racket. Her blond braid whipped against her T-back tank, and the pleats on her teeny-tiny kick-skirt opened and shut accordion style. "How are you going to be pro if so lazy? And why so colorful? This is not circus."

But Dylan was unsinkable. Her crush was starting to crush back. And that's what really mattered.

"I was with J.T!" She twirled, scuffing the dusty clay.

"Good. So we are done. Give me phone and I will erase." She held out her callused palm and wiggled her fingers.

Dylan jumped back. "Not a chance. I may have the look down but I still have a lot to learn. We're going to a match tomorrow and I need to know—"

"The junior club champion Brady Erickson?" Svetlana smashed another ball, narrowly missing a sparrow soaring overhead.

"Yup." Dylan twirled again, loving the feeling of the Hawaiian sun on her face. "He asked me."

"Dressed like *that*?" Svetlana snickered.

Yes!" Dylan felt a surge of anger.

"Hardtobelieve," Svetlana mumbled. "Now, let's start."

Svetlana stomped toward the center of the court, suddenly all business. "This is net." She whacked the black mesh with the side of her Wilson.

"Nyet?" Dylan giggled.

Svetlana rolled her blue-green eyes.

"And this is tennis court." Svetlana kicked the clay. "This is baseline. This is ball."

"Got it. Now let's move on to the advanced stuff." Dylan squatted over the baseline, bent her knees, and wiggled her butt. "Serve it up!"

"Oh-kay." Svetlana jogged to the other side. She arched her back, threw the ball into the air, and swung. "Huuu-waugh!"

Dylan squeezed her eyes shut and waved her racket wildly in all directions. To her surprise, she made contact. Only, it felt like she had slammed into a speeding Hummer.

"Owie!" She opened her eyes, then wiggled her arm to make sure it was still attached. The clay around her was littered with red crystals.

"Whoops!" Svetlana smiled, not looking the least bit sorry. She took another ball out of her pocket and rocked back and forth on her heels, preparing to serve.

"Wait! Stop." Dylan tried to lift her palm, but her shoulder rang out in pain. "I'm injured."

"You've only hit one ball." Svetlana lowered her racket.

Dylan feebly pulled her blackmail LG from the teeny-tiny pocket sewn into her colorful wrap dress as she stumbled over to the sideline. "Get me a masseuse, aysap!"

Svetlana released the ball. It rolled to the side of the court and slammed up against the cool metal chain-link fence.

Just like Dylan.

Dylan finally found the strength she needed to stand. She smoothed her skirt and caught a flattering glimpse of her toned quads. Amazing how quickly they were responding to her tennis training.

The Hawaiian sun reflected off the clay and into her green eyes. For a moment she couldn't see across the court, but she could hear the ball whizzing toward her. She stepped back, pivoted right, pulled her glittering racket back, and swung. *Swoosh!* The ball glided effortlessly over the net as she completed her gazelle-like follow-through.

"Brilliant shot!" a male voice called.

Male voice? Where was Svetlana?

A cloud passed in front of the glaring sun. Dylan could see clearly now.

The voice belonged to J.T. His dimples deepened as he grinned in respect.

Dylan smiled her thanks. She popped a ball out of her dress pocket and whipped out her best serve. The ball shot to the exact spot that she'd hoped. *Ace!*

J.T. returned it with a grunt, and they rallied back and forth, trading break points. The game was heating up, yet Dylan remained remarkably cool. Just before she could serve for match point, J.T. dropped his racket and bounded over the net.

"You know this is my side of the court, right?" Dylan teased, her heart beating like a hummingbird's. What was J.T. doing?

"No, I'm pretty sure it's mine." He closed the gap between them, the tips of his Nikes touching her Mint Chocolate Chips.

Ehmagawd!

He leaned closer. Then closer . . . then . . . his Gatorade-soaked lips touched hers.

Her first lip-kiss tasted like a melted Creamsicle, just like she'd always imagined.

The next thing she knew, she and J.T. were walking on the beach drinking virgin Blue Hawaiis with little pink umbrellas and plastic monkeys that hung from the lips of the glasses by their curly brown tails. They crisscrossed arms and drank from each other's straws. Then, with no warning at all, a huge burp blasted forth from Dylan's glossy mouth.

J.T. spit out his straw.

"Ehmagawd, please pretend you didn't hear that," she blush-begged, contemplating diving into the surging ocean to hide her shame.

"I can't." He stepped back.

"No! J.T., wait!" Dylan felt her Blue Hawaii inching back up her throat. She couldn't stand losing another crush to her mouth gas.

"Eccccccchhhhhhh," J.T. belched.

Dylan burst out laughing, then burped again gleefully. He thought it was funny! "JAAAYYYY TEEEEEE!"

"DYYYYYY-LAAAAAAN." He doubled over in hysterics.

Dylan dropped to the sand and rolled around clutching her abs, which were becoming tighter and tighter by the second.

"You're so awesome." He pushed his brown highlights away from his eyes. "I can't believe it took me two whole days to realize it. I was so wrapped up in tennis I didn't realize my perfect match was right here in front of me."

Dylan searched the empty beach for a witness. Not that she needed one—this moment would be so burned in her brain she'd be able to relive it with vivid accuracy for years to come. It would be like pressing repeat on her favorite track, only better.

"How can I make it up to you?" J.T. dropped to his knees.

"What about a massage?" Dylan flicked off her red dress straps.

"Did I ever tell you how much I like your outfit?" He gripped her tanned shoulders. "It's so vibrant."

Dylan lowered her head, giving him complete access to her neck.

He rubbed. "It shows you have style and confidence. Anyone can follow the herd and wear white. But you're a leader. And that's hot."

She sighed and closed her eyes. "Oh, J.T. . . ."

"Who is J.T.?" snapped a woman with a terse Russian accent. "I'm Simca."

Dylan's eyes flew open. The hand on her back wasn't J.T.'s.

It belonged to a big blond Amazon whose blocklike torso cast a shadow on the wall that resembled that of SpongeBob SquarePants. She was wide awake now. Gone were the secluded beach, the romantic burping contest, and her crushing-back crush. Instead, she was stretched out on her belly in Svetlana's humid bungalow, wearing nothing but a towel. Her red braid had been tightly pinned to the top of her head and was pulling her raw scalp rawer.

"Count to three." Simca hoisted up Dylan's injured arm.

"Wait, why?" Dylan lifted her head, but Simca shoved it back down.

"Count!"

Dylan whimpered, "One . . . two . . ."

Crack!

"OWWWWWW," she wailed.

She buried her sweaty face in the plush towel below her face and tried to catch her breath, shoulder throbbing and heart aching.

J.T. punched his fist in the air. "Another ace!"

Everyone in the Dalys' box set down their mimosas and applauded while Dylan sighed and checked her LG.

Time: 10 a.m.

Google Maps location: Hell.

She and J.T. were pressed up against the window in his family's luxury box, surrounded by John Senior's white-wearing cronies. To the fans below they must have looked like a cluster of cotton balls jammed inside one of those glass jars.

Not the most romantic setting or the best-dressed crowd or the coolest first-date activity, but definitely the cutest guy.

Definitely.

Dylan's gloss was thick and reflective, and her long, super-straight red hair had been tightly side-braided thanks to Ingrid. She'd chosen a belted T-shirt slouch dress in bright ivory—a subtle attempt to stand out, not stick out. She'd even stuck crème brûlée–scented sneaker packs in her Forty-Loves so a waft of vanilla would follow her wherever she happened to tread.

But for some reason, J.T. was Brady-drooling much more

than he was Dylan-drooling, which made posing as a psyched-to-be-here spectator extremely difficult.

This was even more boring than the Briarwood soccer games. At least there, the Pretty Committee would kill time gossiping and game-crushing on the players. But here, she and J.T. weren't even allowed to whisper. Aloha rules insisted on absolute silence while the ball was in play. And thanks to Brady's "Mach ten serve and slammin' forehand" (J.T.'s terms, nawt Dylan's), that ball was *always* in play.

Shifting in her Forty-Loves (and emitting a pouf of vanilla), Dylan decided to use the silence rule to her advantage. She leaned in close to J.T., inhaled, and seductively whispered, "Is that Dior Homme?"

"No, pomegranateproteinsmoothie," he speed-whispered back, his eyes fixed on Brady as he raced to return Karl Sveningson's powerful serve. "Ourboxattendantwillgetyouoneifyouwant."

"Um, no, that's okay. I'm good." Dylan sighed and took a sip of her Perrier.

"Yessss!" J.T. happy-hissed, looking down at the court. "Beautiful!"

Dylan tried to imagine he was talking about her, but couldn't manage to convince herself. Even her fantasies knew better.

Regrouping, she moved on to tactic number two. Petting her snake-braid, she lifted her elbow so that it grazed the side of his sweat-wicking Nike crewneck. The contact sent crush-shivers down her self-tanned arm and a shock of pain through her tender shoulder. Still, J.T. did not look away from the match. Maybe his shirt wicked away flirtatious advances as well.

Finally, Dylan tried to watch the game with the focus of a true die-hard. It would have helped if Svetlana had loaded her up with some in-the-know phrases, but Dylan wasn't afraid to improvise. The more she watched Brady pivot his way around the clay, the more she understood the reasons behind J.T.'s athlete crush.

Brady's curly black hair was tied in a mini-ponytail—an *ah-dorably* rebellious move for someone in such a J. Crew–cut-loving profession—and his deep tan and sweat-slicked muscles gleamed like a patent leather Coach handbag. According to Merri-Lee's info, he'd landed the Prince endorsement, a three-episode run on *The Young and the Restless,* and had been making the rounds of the talk-show circuit. But still, he was no Zac Efron. More like Adam Brody with a body. Which was far from a bad thing . . .

"Ughhhh." He grunt-whipped the ball right into the net, which shook from the force.

"Yeah, Brady, that's what I'm talkin' about!" Dylan banged loudly on the glass.

J.T. grabbed her arms and quickly lowered them, sneaking a quick look back at his dad. "What are you *doing*?!"

Dylan's shoulder had flared up with fiery pain when he grabbed her. But so what? He was holding her wrists!

J.T.'s pearl-clad mother shifted in the seat behind Dylan.

"Did you see how hard he hit that?" Dylan beamed. "What a swing!"

J.T. looked confused, like he'd been suddenly roused from a deep sleep. "Brady *lost* the point."

Uh-oh.

"I thought you were a *fan*!" Dylan tried, her mind running for an explanation.

"I am." J.T. still looked confused.

"Then you should support him no matter what," she whisper-hissed, rolling her eyes for added punch.

J.T. looked away for a moment, probably to consider this. Seconds later, a huge smile spread across his Twizzler-red lips. "Wow."

Score. Dylan had actually made him reevaluate the sport while forcing him to contemplate the true meaning of—

"Is that Svetlana?"

Dylan sucked in her abs and panic-scanned the spectators below. It wasn't long before she spotted the blonde in her ultra-low V-neck LWTD. She was sidestepping her way across a row of bleachers, clueless to the tongues that wagged as she squeezed by. Stopping at the only empty courtside seat, she pinch-grabbed the warm-up jacket that had been intentionally left as a placeholder, released it to the ground, and sat. Once settled, she lifted the Aloha Open visor off her head and unleashed her flowing waves slow-mo style. *What happened to the braid? And the straight hair?* Svetlana looked like Dylan *before* the mind-numbing, four-hour transformation. And now it would be months before the chemicals wore off and her own curls popped back. Pure evil!

Svetlana's eyes scanned the crowd. A devious smile

cracked its way across her taut face when she located the Daly box and realized J.T. was watching her. She winked her faux lashes at him and crossed her oil-slicked legs with slow determination, as though they were underwater.

J.T. exhaled longingly, leaving a steam cloud of desire on the glass.

Opposite of acceptable! Svetlana was ah-bviously doing this to mess with Dylan. Well, a quick shake of her LG should put a stop to that. And it did. Svetlana's shoulders dropped slightly. She put her visor back on, coyly lowered it over her blue-green eyes, and focused on the match.

Seconds later, the cheering crowd tipped Dylan off to a successful swing by Brady. "That was some backhandler!" she shouted.

J.T. whipped around to face her.

Direct eye contact. Finally! She had his full attention now.

"Are you even watching the same match as I am?" His brow furrowed.

Nervous heat starting pricking under her pits, and Dylan hoped desperately that her freesia-scented deodorant would keep the crisis in check.

"Of course I'm watching the same match. Now *shhhh*!" she chided him, desperate to change the topic.

"You do know there's no such thing as a backhandler, right? It's called a *backhand*."

Outside, polite applause followed a loud tennis-grunt.

"I *know*. That's just our nickname for them back at the Westchester Tennis Club."

J.T. crossed his arms. "You *look* like you're really into tennis, but it seems like you don't actually know anything about it. I mean—"

Dylan forced herself to face his disapproving eyes. "I'll show you how into tennis I am when Svetlana and I play later this week."

J.T. gasped. "Are you serious?"

"If by serious you mean *stupid*, then ah-bso-lutely," Dylan wanted to say.

But instead she sigh-nodded yes and smiled awkwardly, the way love-struck girls often do.

"This will only take a sec." Dylan pushed past Svetlana and charged into the tennis phenom's humid bungalow that afternoon. An image of the athlete midserve, looking constipated, was frozen on the plasma.

"Ehmagawd!" Dylan giggled "No wonder you didn't want me to come in. You were checking out your grunt face."

"I admit nothing." Svetlana held the remote over her white-robed shoulder and clicked the TV off.

"Whatevs." Dylan helped herself to one of the Svetlana for Luna bars on the mahogany coffee table. "Anyway, we'll be playing a match in five days, and I need you to let me kick your highly downloaded butt." She admired her blue and silver striped tank dress in the star-shaped wall mirror. The slight A-line was perfect for size sixes posing as fours.

Svetlana took a hearty gulp of green Gatorade. "Ahhhhh!" She lobbed the empty jug into a wicker plant holder by the living area.

Gawd! Didn't Svetlana need to burp after a chug like that? What was it about sexy blondes and their lack of gas? Maybe beauty wasn't skin-deep. Perhaps it ran deeper.

"So, are you in?" Dylan asked.

"Hmmmm." Svetlana lifted the napping Boris out of the

white-brick fireplace and began scratching his tiny head with her ultra-square acrylic tips. "What is point of this deception?"

"J.T. will be watching. And if he sees me beat you, he will believe I am a tennis goddess." She rubbed the dull ache in her shoulder.

"Svetlana has doubts." She tucked a silky blond wave behind her ear.

Dylan tried to do the same with her stiff red braid. It was like trying to twirl raw spaghetti.

"I cannot throw a game." She scratched Boris harder. "Even for silly pretend match."

"Cannot? Or *will* not?" Dylan dared.

"Both. Is bad for career." She stood firm, her unpedicured feet planted on the beige sisal rug.

"So is votive throwing in a meditation chamber." Dylan waved her phone.

Svetlana closed her eyes and exhaled slowly. Dylan wiped her sweat-drenched palms on the side of her striped dress.

"Fine." Svetlana hate-squinted, her taut lips flattened into a fine line.

Done! Dylan stuffed the phone back in her silver sequin–covered tennis bag. Just as she was about to zip it shut, Svetlana tossed Boris on the bed and lunged at her with cougar-like ferocity.

Reee-owwwww!

"Back off!" Dylan quickly shielded her bag like a precious newborn. She shook her head in disgust while she waited for her racing heart to settle. "Try that again and your new sponsor will be *Done*-lop."

Svetlana took a step back. "Fine. But I have three conditions."

Dylan opened her mouth to protest, but Svetlana quickly covered it with her callused hand. "I have three conditions." She held up her long index finger. "One. You erase the veedyo the second the match is over."

"Agreed." Dylan pushed down her finger.

"Two. No one will believe you can beat me if they don't see you train."

Dylan suddenly became painfully aware that her inner thighs were touching. "Point?"

"We train. Then, on the court, you do what I say when I say it. I have trademark-pending regimen to ensure success. So it will be the Svetlana Way™ all the way. Yes?" She handed Dylan a foldout pamphlet detailing the training philosophy.

"Yes." Dylan rolled her emerald green eyes and stuffed the pamphlet into her racket bag. "And three?"

"No. Compliments. Ever."

"You mean *complaints*?" Dylan asked, assuming Svetlana was still working on her three-syllable words. After all, compliments were the *only* reason to work out.

"No. I mean *compliments*." Her nostrils flared slightly, showing that she meant business. "None. Not one. Ever."

Dylan suddenly remembered Winsome mentioning something about Svetlana and compliments, but the details were fuzzy. She'd been in a color-induced haze that day. She considered asking Svetlana why, but decided against it. The opportunity to spend the day with a gorgeous, athletic superstar and not have to feed her ego seemed like a real bonus. "No prob. Now, do we have a deal?"

Svetlana flopped onto her bed and shoved Boris in the cubby of space between her neck and chin. They both stared mournfully at the rattan ceiling fan. "We have deal."

Dylan smirked. She might not know a thing about tennis, but she was an expert at playing the game.

Diing-donng.

Dylan curled into extreme fetal and pulled the honeysuckle-scented duvet over her head. Did her early-bird mother have to catch the worm *every* morning?

Diiing-donnng.

She lifted the pink silk eye mask over her limp red hair and lifted her LG. Four A.M.! Dylan lowered the mask and turned her pillow over to the cold side.

Diiiing-donnnnnnnng.

"Maaaaa! Cassidy's here."

"Who is Cassidy?" shouted a distant but familiar voice.

Dylan whipped off her eye mask and tiptoed out of her room. Merri-Lee was sound asleep in the master suite wearing giant Bose headphones, her silicone-filled chest rising and falling like the buoys that bobbed on the surf beneath their window.

Stumbling over the cool marble to the dimly lit foyer, Dylan reached for the door, accidentally knocking the continental breakfast menu off the handle.

"What?" She finally managed to open it.

Clad in white short-shorts and a puff-sleeved hoodie, Svetlana was tapping her foot, a silver whistle lodged between her pursed lips.

Purrrrp!

"Shhhhhh." Dylan searched the dark, secluded grounds. Not even the happy island birds were chirping at this hour. "What are you doing?"

"We train." Svetlana had tied her damp, wavy hair into a high pony. "Let's go."

"Is this some kind of weird tennis hazing ritual or something?" Dylan grumbled. "What about breakfast?"

PUURRRPPPPPP!

The chain-link-fence door to the private courts slammed shut behind them, sending a reverberating *clang* through the lazy resort. The air was dark and chilly. In the distance the surf roared something that sounded like *sleeeep . . . sleeeep . . . sleeeep . . .* Dylan's stomach grumbled, her eyes burned, and a screeching bat was circling her tangled red extensions. Just as she was about to call it quits, Dylan considered J.T.'s Efron-esque features and quickly concluded that this would eventually be worth it.

"Surrender!" Svetlana shouted as she bear-hugged Dylan and squeezed.

"Ahhhhhh! Helllllp!" Dylan pleaded, but her morning voice was hoarse and weak.

"Got it!" Svetlana triumphantly pulled a chocolate chip oatmeal cookie from the pocket of Dylan's yellow cotton dress. "This is not part of the Svetlana Way™! Read pamphlet!" She tossed the cookie in the air and slammed it to bits with her racket.

Dylan's stomach cried out in protest. She considered dropping and doing her best DustBuster impression when—

Puuurrrrrp!

"Do like I do." Svetlana pushed play on her Bose docking station and began darting across the court. Classical music mashed with a thumping bass blasted at maximum volume.

Dylan stared longingly at the cookie crumbs.

"Now!" Svetlana barked from across the court. "Or I will tell everyone you are size *six*!"

"How do you know *that*?" Dylan jogged lightly. "My labels say four."

"Winsome works for me, remember?" Svetlana smirked, clearly happy to finally have a leg up. "This is only way to be real four!" She lifted her whistle to her lips. "Now run, NoodleLegs!"

PUUURPPP!

"Fine!" Dylan began sprinting, fueled at first by humiliation and then by determination. Imagine! If she became a four, she could finally tell people she was a two.

The girls ran until the rising sun turned the sky orange—like juice and marmalade and cheddar. . . .

And then Dylan collapsed on the baseline, dry heaving and pinching up cookie crumbs.

Before she was ready to stand—*pop!*—Svetlana hit her first serve.

"Wait! I wasn't ready," Dylan yelled from the baseline

Pop! Another ball whizzed by Dylan's diamond-studded ear.

"That's two," Svetlana called.

Pop! Dylan jumped up and swung blindly.

"Three."

"Wait, why are you counting?" She lowered her racket.

"Every time you miss a ball, there's a consequence. Clearly you didn't read about the Svetlana Way™ carefully enough. For that, I add five minutes of sprinting. Now go!"

Dylan blinked. "You've got to be kidding."

"Do you want boy or not?"

Dylan sighed and jogged to the net. She slapped its white plastic top, then headed back to the baseline—again and again and again.

The minute she was done, Svetlana wound up for her next serve.

Pop!

This time, the strings on Dylan's racket connected with Svetlana's ball. It floated away from Dylan and sailed up, up, up in the air and over the fence.

"Sah-ree!" She turned back to Svetlana, who did not look amused.

"Drop and give me twenty-five," she barked.

"But you told me to leave my wallet in the bungalow." Dylan pulled out her pockets to show she didn't have any cash, and a flurry of cookie crumbs dusting the courts.

"Twenty-five push-ups, Size *Six*!"

"Don't call me—"

Puuuurp.

Dylan sighed, assuming the push-up position. Her palms,

which were unaccustomed to carrying anything heavier than a patent leather Chloé Paddington, were not prepared to handle this much Dylan. After two feeble attempts, her elbows buckled and her injured shoulder attempted suicide. She collapsed face-first into a Nike shoe print.

"All we have to do is fake a match. This is a little much, don'tcha think?"

"You can't *fake* tennis." Svetlana slammed her racket down on the net. "Now, twenty-three to go."

Dylan took a deep breath, placed her palms back on the red clay, and pushed herself up twenty-three more times in the name of love.

"Now for the serve." Svetlana pulled a ball out of her pocket and threw it at Dylan.

Miraculously, she caught the ball and began running in place like she'd seen Svetlana do before her serves.

"Weight on front foot, watch that stance, and breathe! Like this." Svetlana tossed the ball in the air and whipped it across the court.

Dylan cheer-clapped. "Wow, that was amaz—"

PUUURP!

"No compliments!" Svetlana shouted. "Now you." She aimed a speed gun at Dylan.

Dylan, feeling thinner already, dribbled the ball a few times on the clay. She threw it toward the cloudless sky and swung her racket up to meet it. "Huu-ahhhh!"

Pop! The ball sailed over the net.

"Yay! That was pretty good, huh?" Dylan beamed, reminding her mentor that the no-compliment rule did not apply to her.

Svetlana checked the speed gun. "Eleven miles per hour. Unbelievable."

"Almost the speed limit in a school zone. I must be a natural." Dylan rocked excitedly on the heels of her silver Nikes.

"No, I mean it's *not* believable. And we need it to be believable or no one will think you can beat me. I serve a 129. Now, again."

From the baseline, Dylan could see surfers riding the shimmering waves. She wanted to be on the beach taking their pictures and forwarding her Roxy moment to the Pretty Committee. Instead, she sighed and threw another ball up in the air. Imagining Svetlana's smug face on the fuzzy lime-green Wilson, she whacked it as hard as she could.

Pop!

Svetlana looked at the speed gun again. "Not as awful."

They practiced serves for another hour under the hot Hawaiian sun.

"Enough!" Svetlana announced.

"Finally!" Dylan dropped to her knees. "I need some carbs and a wardrobe change."

"Nyet." Svetlana tossed her a pair of white patent leather stilettos with rubber traction soles. "Put these on, Flatfoot."

"Nyet way!" Dylan jumped back. "Those aren't shoes— they're *ews*."

"You must. It will teach you how to stay on your toes." She thrust the shoes toward Dylan's face.

"I have some ah-dorable snakeskin Marnis that will do the trick." Dylan waved the nurse-gone-naughty pumps away like stinky poi. She'd heard Svetlana's mom-coach had unorthodox ways of creating the tennis terminator, but this was inhumane. "How 'bout we break for lunch and I'll bring them for our afternoon session?"

"Marion Bartoli's papa used to tape tennis balls to the soles of her feet," Svetlana reported. "And Pussycat Dolls run on treadmill wearing four-inch clogs."

"What?"

"No what." Svetlana dropped the offending white pumps on the court. They bounced twice, then settled by Dylan's feet. "Do you want this J.T. to think you are good player, or do you want him to know you are Sizesix Flatfoot NoodleLeg Loserfan?"

"I said, no more names!" Dylan grabbed the heels and jammed them on her swollen feet. The patent leather was hard and unforgiving, just like Svetlana.

She stood with the awkward wobble of a newborn giraffe.

"Break's over!" Svetlana yelled from across the court, loading different-colored tennis balls into the serving machine. "Stand on baseline. Prepare to hit."

Dylan assumed the position, doing her best to balance. But the combination of the springy sole, tough leather, and three-inch heels made her feel like she had two pogo sticks jammed through the soles of her feet. Tennis was hard enough in Nikes!

"Ready?" Svetlana pressed a button and a rainbow of balls shot directly at Dylan. Pink. Blue. Red. Yellow. Orange.

Lavender. Pink. Blue. Red. Yellow. Orange. Lavender. Pink. Blue. Red. Yellow. Orange. Lavender. Pink. Blue. Red. Yellow. Orange. Lavender.

"AAAAAAhhhhhh!" Dylan racket-blocked her face. But the barrage of balls pelted her entire body and knocked her to the ground. She lay flat, spread out like a facedown snow angel.

Finally, the balls stopped. Dylan managed to stand back up, her entire body stinging and throbbing.

"Ready?" Svetlana yelled, not waiting for the answer. "Here comes red ball!"

Dylan swung but missed.

"Yellow!"

Dylan swung again and teetered. She missed the ball but didn't fall down—a victory by her standards.

"Now green!" Svetlana pressed the trigger again.

Dylan stumble-ran for the ball. She missed this one, too.

"Blue!"

The balls came faster and faster, and Svetlana yelled louder and louder.

"Purple!" But she could barely swing anymore.

"Let's go, you size six . . ."

Dylan could see Svetlana's lips moving as she yelled, but all she could hear was a loud buzz. Her arms prickled with heat and her mouth felt like it was wrapped around a blasting hair dryer. She dropped her glittery racket and signaled T for time out before collapsing on the hot clay.

"Get up!" Svetlana called somewhere in the distance. "Up, up, up . . ."

But the only thing that rose were the illegal oatmeal chocolate chip cookie crumbs. They came up, up, up . . . all over Svetlana's white Nikes.

"Ani-maaaal!" Svetlana roared, kicking off her shoes.

Beads of something wet trickled down Dylan's cheeks. She was so spent she couldn't tell if it was sweat or tears or left-over puke.

Finally, as she lay helpless on the steamy ground, she called out for something white. It was the flag of surrender. And in her buzzing brain she was waving it.

Hard.

Dylan was wrapped up like a spicy tuna hand roll in her 100-thread-count duvet, longingly eyeing a banana split as it floated toward her dry mouth. Placed in the center of a shiny silver tray, it was surrounded by an aura of fuzzy light as if it had been sent from heaven just for her. Just as the angel—dressed in a burgundy room service uniform—set it down on the table next to the bed, a callused hand with square-tipped acrylic French-manicured nails waved it away.

"She'll have ginger ale," a commanding voice instructed.

The angel and her tray turned abruptly and headed for the door.

"Wait . . ." Dylan mumbled feebly.

But it was too late. The split had split.

"It's all for better," the voice boomed. This time there was no mistaking the thick accent or gruff delivery.

Svetlana was perched on the edge of the bed, stroking Boris, who was purring in her lap. She mowed her square nails through his fur, from butt to head, making it spike up like a Mohawk. A can of ginger ale was in her other hand.

"What are *you* doing here?" Dylan shot up in horror. The uneven bamboo slats on the headboard dug into her throbbing back and woke her pain, taking it from a seven point five to a raging nine.

"Open." Svetlana poked the bendy straw between Dylan's cracked lips, then crossed her legs. She was wearing J Brand pencil-leg jeans and a blue and red striped Vince tank. Her blond hair was in a loose side-pony that overflowed with deep-conditioned curls. She looked like a regular girl. "Sip."

Dylan found the cold fizz invigorating and drained the can in a single gulp.

"Thanks," she whisper-burped. But her relief was temporary. All of a sudden her heart thumped in a post-espresso sort of way and her skin prickled with the sting of adrenaline. "My phone!" She patted down her thighs like a frisking cop. "Where's my . . ." The hard rectangular object digging into her hip meant it was right where she left it, in her side pocket. "Oh."

Thank Gawd! She pulled it out and gripped it between her stiff fingers.

"You know," Svetlana said, tracing the beading on a ruby red Indian silk throw pillow, "I was not always this perfect. I had hard times training too."

Boris yawned. Dylan rolled her eyes.

"Back in Russia, when I was six-year-old, Mom-Coach would pull me off cot at four in morning so we could claim public court before anyone else. This court had no room behind baseline, so if I swung wide I'd smash wall and break flesh. Then blood from my knuckles would freeze from cold." She showed Dylan her scars. "But Mom-Coach made me stick with it. It was our way out."

Dylan imagined little Svetlana in the dark winter mornings, bashing her fists into the cracked concrete while her frozen baby braid stabbed her hypothermic cheeks like an ice pick.

"So I didn't think today's lesson was hard. Because for me, spacious court in hot Hawaiian sun with proper-fitting shoes seemed easy."

"Um, your cookie-covered Nikes should prove it was the opposite of *easy*."

"*Nyet.*" Svetlana placed Boris on the marble floor and dabbed her tearing eyes with the bottom of her tank top. "Opposite of *easy* is when Mom-Coach would chase me on Vespa, making me run ten miles every day in bitter cold along Neva River. I ate nothing but hard-boiled eggs and bread for eleven years. Friends, school, boy crushes, colorful clothes—I never had time."

Dylan sighed, remembering that horrible afternoon in the sixth grade when she gave up carbs. Her energy had been super-low, and she'd snapped more times than a Splendid button-front cardigan. And what if she didn't have Massie's Friday night sleepovers to look forward to? Or the Pretty Committee's GLU meetings? Or gossip points? Or crushes? Or shopbop.com?

"It can't possibly be worth it." Dylan siphoned the excess ginger ale from the straw. "Why didn't you tell Mom-Coach you wanted to stop?"

Svetlana shrugged. "Every time I wanted to quit, I'd imagine winning and having money so family could move to America, get heated home, and train in real facility. It was only way that pudgy little six-year-old was going to make it to Wimbledon. And once I did, I—"

Dylan crushed the empty can. "Wait, rewind. You were *fat*?"

"Da. Svetlana could pinch an inch." She placed her hand gently on Dylan's duvet-covered knee. "See? You and me—we are not so different."

"Why? You think *I'm* fat?" Her cheeks burned with trepidation.

Svetlana shook her head dismissively, as if that was so not the point. "When I made it to Wimbledon, I *had* to win. Not only for me, or Mom-Coach, or my country. But for all things I sacrificed along the way. Winning meant I didn't give all up for nothing."

Dylan was starting to feel for the tennis star. And then her stomach grumbled. Suddenly, all she could think about was that banana split and how if she were eating it she'd be a lot more captivated by this *E! True Hollywood* moment.

"I was *this* close to winning second year in row," Svetlana continued, oblivious to Dylan's hunger-rebellion. Her blue-green eyes darted back and forth as though she were watching the match in real time. "The ball had been served and I was in perfect position to slam." Svetlana drew back her arm as though she were about to whack it. "Then, out of nowhere, random loserfan yelled, 'Svetlana, you rock!' I lost concentration. I missed ball. I lost Wimbledon." Svetlana's buff shoulders sagged. "And ball girl paid price."

"Is that why you don't like compliments?" Dylan wondered, recalling her earlier conversation with Winsome.

Svetlana sad-nodded yes.

Dylan reached out to pat her hand. She couldn't help

herself—the athlete looked so upset and vulnerable. Until now, all Dylan had seen was Svetlana's utterly enviable life— filled with trophies, endorsement deals, personal stylists, and zero-percent body fat. But now she knew better. Svetlana's knuckle scars, compliment issues, and egg overdose made her Dr. Phil–worthy. And that meant she was just as messed up as everyone else. It was a total relief.

"One question." Dylan began nibbling on her pinky nail. "When you said we weren't so different, were you talking about weight or—"

"Not weight." Svetlana pulled her hand out from under Dylan's and dried her moist blue-green eyes. "We both have things we want. And we both work hard to get them."

"Yeah, but . . ." Dylan sighed. "There's no way I'll ever be good enough to convince J.T. I can beat you."

"Good point." Svetlana tucked American Boris under her arm and stood up. "So then we drop this whole thing, ya?" She held out her palm, as if Dylan would just slap her LG into it like a bellboy's tip.

All four chambers of Dylan's open heart slammed shut. If this sob story was just another attempt to get her hands on that video file, she was messing with the wrong girl.

"We drop nothing!" Dylan threw off her duvet and cracked her non-bloody knuckles. It was time to get serious.

Svetlana might have trained during the harsh Russian winters with Mom-Coach, but Dylan had studied under Massie Block. And that had prepared her for *anything*.

Even tennis.

Dylan pored over the Svetlana Way™ pamphlet like it was a *How to Get J.T. for Dummies* handbook.

Visualize.

Actualize.

Vocalize.

The mental exercises made her feel a little, well, *mental,* but she was desperate. As the July 8 tournament date grew closer, the resort was bouncing with toned and tanned she-athletes. And Dylan knew if she didn't score J.T. soon, someone else would.

Reaching for a lemon yellow microfiber towel, she accidentally knocked the pamphlet to the ground. All she could do was grunt in frustration and swab her slick face. Still, sweat spilled over her arched auburn brows like the water that trickled down the spa's pink travertine walls.

She was hot. She'd never been this hot, and she had to concentrate on every breath or she'd faint. *In, out. In, out. In, out . . .*

Once she got a rhythm going, Dylan allowed her mind to wander.

How hard would J.T. lip-kiss her after she creamed Svetlana? How open would he be to a four-thousand-mile long-distance relationship? Was he a texter?

Throwing the towel aside, Dylan exhaled, utterly exhausted.

It was taking every ounce of her will and concentration to keep from passing out. After a long sip of cucumber water, she decided to go for it. She reached and reached and reached . . . until her fingers managed to pinch the corner of the Svetlana Way™ pamphlet she'd accidentally dropped on the sauna room floor.

Got it!

She pulled it back up onto her steamy lap, careful not to let the fuchsia ink rub off on her sweat-drenched thighs. Not that it really mattered. It would rinse right off in the pool.

Once the hairy-chested man with the gold rings and red bathing cap was halfway down the lane, Dylan pushed off the slippery cobalt blue–tiled edge. The indoor lap pool was heated to bathtub temperatures and teeming with serious swimmers who slapped the chlorinated water with their tired strokes like mindless aqua-zombies. Splashes and random coughs echoed up to the glass roof and ricocheted off the limestone walls, making Dylan feel like an exotic fish in a very luxurious tank.

Gliding as hard as she could, Dylan finally reached the other side and burst to the surface. She wall-clung momentarily to admire the beading water on her silver Robin Piccone one-piece, which glistened like a sardine in the sunshine. If only J.T. were into fashion instead of tennis . . .

But the Svetlana Way™ emphasized not living in a fantasyland. Success was not about what ifs. It was about what nexts. So Dylan took a deep breath and submerged for lap number two.

The hollow sound of her underwater heartbeat provided a rhythmic backdrop for her J.T. musings.

Thump-thump. Thump-thump. Thump-thump. Jyl-an. Jyl-an. Jyl-an.

It didn't have the ring of Brangelina or Tomkat, but it wasn't awful.

Dylan straddled the black nylon workout bench. Her forehead crinkled under the strain of her task. Yet somehow, she managed to lift a bottle of SmartWater to her dry lips.

"Uggghhh!" she moaned. The angle ravaged her sore shoulder and sent shock waves of pain up her arm.

This warm-up session was o-*ver*.

"Did you warm up?" Svetlana asked when she met up with Dylan outside the fitness center. Dylan's cheeks were flushed with post-practice sweat, and her chest rose and fell like a panting dog's.

"I did." Dylan squinted against the afternoon sun. She felt like she had just crawled out of a cave. The tropical grounds seemed saturated in color compared with the steel-gray and black weight room. Once again, she had to ask herself if J.T. was worth sacrificing sun, sand, and seafood. And once again, her answer was yes.

"Here is itinerary for the next two days. We have match on

day three." Svetlana handed Dylan a piece of hotel stationery filled with her slanted, all-caps handwriting. The back of the paper felt like bumpy Braille because the rage-filled athlete had pushed too hard with the pen.

THE SVETLANA WAY™ TWO-DAY SCHEDULE

6 A.M.–8 A.M.:	5-MILE RUN WITH PEBBLE IN SHOE
8:05 A.M.–8:15 A.M.:	20 PUSH-UPS WITH SVETLANA ON YOUR BACK
8:19 A.M.–8:58 A.M.:	1,000 CRUNCHES OR 100 WITH MEDICINE BALL—YOU CHOOSE
9 A.M.–10:30 A.M.:	WEIGHT ROOM CIRCUIT, NO WATER
10:35 A.M.–4 P.M.:	TENNIS DRILLS, BALL MACHINE, HIGH-HEEL SPRINTS. THIS INCLUDES A SHORT HALF-HOUR LUNCH OF HARD-BOILED EGG AND GATORADE (I CHOOSE FLAVOR)
4:02 P.M.–4:30 P.M.:	YOGA
4:34 P.M.–5:30 P.M.:	MEDITATION IN MOSQUITO-FILLED ROOM
5:36 P.M.–7 P.M.:	2-MILE COOL-DOWN JOG (NO PEBBLE)
7:06 P.M.–8:00 P.M.:	DINNER OF MIXED GREENS, 1/2 BOILED CHICKEN BREAST, GATORADE (YOU CHOOSE FLAVOR)
8:01 P.M.–8:25 P.M.:	REVIEW TENNIS MATCHES ON TV TO AID VISUALIZATION
8:30 P.M.:	SLEEP IN HEAT-FILLED ROOM

Dylan was about to protest but stopped herself. For once in her life she would try. Really try. Relentlessly-refuse-to-fail try. The way Massie did. And her mother did. And Svetlana did. The way winners did.

"I can't believe you two actually *play* together." J.T. looked shyly at the crushed seashell path that led to Private Court One. The collar on his white Lacoste was popped, surrounding his deliciously tanned face like a flour tortilla.

"Most people don't challenge me the way she does, you know?" Dylan playfully kicked a peach-colored shell so J.T. could admire her taut leg muscles in action. After two days of enduring the Svetlana Way™, Dylan felt toned, slim, and 100 percent ready for her faux match. Her indigo puff-sleeved pleated minidress and flaming red extensions made her impossible to overlook. She was the color-soaked *Teen Vogue* version of a tennis player—a stylish poser in a beautiful location. All she needed to complete the picture was the hot boyfriend. And that was coming together beautifully.

"Wow. You're cute *and* determined." J.T. paused on the path and smiled. "Fierce combination." He said *fierce* like he meant *sexy*.

If Dylan had known how to do a back handspring, she would have done one right then and there, even if it meant pressing her soft palms against all those jagged shells.

Mission Make J.T. My SBF was well under way. That morning, at *his* request, he'd picked Dylan up at her bungalow.

Then he had offered to carry her glittery racket case. Even his DEC (Direct Eye Contact) was up 80 percent since the beginning of the week, indicating that their first lip-kiss was a mere match point away.

Now all Dylan needed to do was make the tennis game look believable. If she could pull that off, they'd be hanging a DO NAWT DISTURB sign on their poolside umbrella for the rest of the week.

When they reached the cliffside court, J.T. unhooked the fence. He held it open so Dylan could enter first—possibly a ploy to check out her new and improved butt.

"Hey, Svetlana! We're here," Dylan called.

Svetlana, in a white embellished tank and super-short shorts, was stretching on the far side. Dylan smiled to herself, loving how seriously the athlete was taking her role.

Svetlana wave-jogged over to greet them and gave Dylan a big, bone-crushing hug once she arrived. Over Svetlana's super-sculpted shoulder, Dylan locked eyes with J.T. and grinned. She pulled away to make the introductions, and J.T. took it upon himself to extend his hand.

"It's such an honor to meet you."

"Believe me"—Svetlana winked—"the pleasure's all mine. Now we play, ya?"

Once again Dylan thought Svetlana was getting a little too cutesy with her crush. But she refused to let it bring her down. Not when J.T. had escorted her there and offered to carry her bag. Those gestures screamed CRUSHING BACK! And she didn't need *CosmoGIRL!* to tell her that.

J.T. unzipped Dylan's glittering silver bag and presented her with her racket. She leaned in for one last yummy coconut-scented whiff before parting ways.

It was showtime.

Dylan sauntered over to her side of the court, allowing her diffused, glossy red locks to bounce in time with her custom-made, double-soled Nikes. She stepped behind the baseline, took a deep breath, and let her first serve rip. *"Huh-wah!"*

Svetlana returned it easily, and just like they'd practiced, Dylan slammed it back. As planned, Svetlana attempted to return it but failed to make contact with the ball.

"Fifteen-love." J.T. called from the bench. "Very impressive!"

Dylan dropped into a mini-curtsy and then served again.

Huah! She'd practiced her grunt face enough to know it said, "I'm powerful *and* ah-dorable."

Once again, Svetlana returned the ball and Dylan hit it back so that it sailed just past Svetlana's outstretched racket. The game continued to go perfectly, and they hit the ball back and forth several more times while J.T. whooped and hollered from the sideline. Running back and forth, hitting backhands, forehands, and even one overhead smash, Dylan was in the zone. Meanwhile, Svetlana was proving to be a very convincing pretend-loser. Balls flew just out of her reach or landed just long of baseline. She even eked out a few faux-frustrated grunts to make it look real.

After the first set, J.T. shot Dylan the double thumbs-up,

and, feeling brave, she blew him an air kiss. How cute was he, still holding her rhinestone bag?

"You know," Svetlana called cheerfully from the other side of the court, "I think I'm in the mood for a bagel!"

"Me too!" Dylan's insides soared. "But let's play one more set."

Ehmagawd! No more boiled chicken breasts? It was too perfect. J.T. and a bagel in one day! Would she have cream cheese or peanut butter and jelly? Maybe she'd get half and half. Or tuna and—

All of a sudden a ball sliced across the court. Had it been going any faster, it would have experienced time travel.

Dylan jumped out of the way just in time. She took a deep breath and then bent her knees, in preparation for Svetlana's second serve. "Sorry, I wasn't ready," she called. Then she mouthed, "Take it easy," when J.T. wasn't looking.

This time, Svetlana served with less vigor and Dylan was able to return it. But the ball came back with a vengeance. Dylan swung her racket back, but when the strings made contact with the ball, the force sent her reeling backward. She landed right on her newly toned butt.

"Are you okay?" Svetlana jogged to the net.

"Thirty-love." J.T. announced.

Dylan shot her opponent a threatening you-better-not-try-that-again look as she stood and dusted off her cotton indigo skirt. Svetlana assured her with a slight head nod that it wouldn't happen again. Maybe she wanted to make the match look real so Dylan would have a come-from-behind victory, making J.T. fall even harder for her? That had to be it. *Right*?

Svetlana served again.

Pop!

The ball landed right on the service line.

An *ace*.

"Forty-love!" J.T. shouted, gazing at Svetlana with love in his eyes.

Dylan's stomach churned. Something was off.

Svetlana served again, and Dylan stuck her racket out trying to save set point, but Svetlana was there with her hardest forehand yet.

"Owie." The ball clipped Dylan's shin.

"Oops!" Svetlana covered her mouth in mock guilt.

"You did that on purpose!" Dylan yelled. "Approach the net."

Once they were practically nose-to-nose Dylan hissed, "What are you *doing*?"

Waves crashed ashore in the background and slight breeze ruffled through Dylan's hair.

"Winning," Svetlana said casually.

"This is *nawt* what we agreed to." Dylan stomped her silver Nike on the clay court.

Svetlana shrugged.

"You asked for it!" Dylan speed-hobbled to her bag, which J.T. had finally set down behind him. She reached inside for her LG—this time she was fully prepared to push the button. But the phone wasn't in the outside pocket where she'd left it. Her forehead began beading with sweat.

After frantically rooting through the various mesh compartments, she turned the bag inside out and shook it over the clay. One tube of Nars Nude lip gloss and her black room card fell out.

"Looking for this?" J.T. stood above her, holding the LG.

He gave her the phone along with an adorably charming smile.

Dylan smile-thanked him, then scrolled through her files in search of the incriminating videos. But they were all . . . empty. She checked again. And again. And again.

"Ehmagawd, they're gone!"

"*No*! That's *impossible*!" Svetlana snicker-gasped, coming up behind her.

Dylan looked at J.T. He looked down at his navy Nikes.

"But how?"

"You didn't believe cute boy-crush would choose Size Six Pimple Loserfan over me, did you?" Svetlana pivot-turned to retrieve her own bag and sauntered off the court.

"You set me up." Dylan choked back her betrayal-barf once she and J.T. were alone.

"You *lied* to me," he countered, tossing back his caramel locks.

"You used me."

"You duped me."

Dylan searched her reeling mind for something clever to say. But all that came out was the truth.

"You *hurt* me," she whimpered as she tugged on the hem of her indigo skirt.

Without another word, J.T. turned to go.

"Wait . . ." Dylan begged.

J.T. whipped back around. "*What*? You blackmailed a tennis star." His piercing blue eyes seared her tear-streaked cheeks. "The sport has suffered enough bad press already, don'tcha think?"

"In case you don't remember, *Svetlana's* the one who knocked someone's teeth out." Dylan mimed Svetlana's highly documented de-toothing swing.

"She lost her temper out of love for the game."

"Well, I lost my mind out of love for you!" Dylan considered shouting. But that was too cheesy. Even for a summer romance.

Just then Svetlana returned to the court, swinging her bag and holding two bottles of Voss. She tossed one to J.T. "I know this is probably hard for Pimple to understand, but *bagel* is tennis term describing game where loser stays at love."

"But—"

"You said you wanted love." Svetlana smiled proudly. "Now you got it." She linked her arm through J.T.'s and gave Dylan a big goodbye wave.

Left on the sidelines, Dylan hated herself. She hated boys, athletes, and bright Hawaiian sunshine. Why did everyone get to be happy but her? Even Tennis the Menace—a violent psychopath—found a crush who crushed back.

She whipped her LG onto the court and felt nothing as she watched it shatter.

Had she been insane to think J.T. would believe she was a

tennis buff? Or had she been insane for *wanting* him to believe it? After all, those imperfection-loving Dove soap commercials told her to be proud of the girl she was. To own and luhv her flaws and quirks and wear them on her size-six sleeves with pride. If those ads had lasted more than thirty seconds, they'd have told her she was she was much better off alone. Because pretending to be someone you weren't could never make you happy. And now she knew the truth about J.T.'s feelings, right? She should be relieved, right? Almost grateful she hadn't wasted another second trying to be someone she wasn't, right?

WRONG!

She was tired of being strong. Tired of smiling though the pain. Maybe one day *Maxim* would want a burping, size-six redhead on its cover. But until then Dylan decided to slouch back to her bungalow, order room service, and mend her broken heart with sticky butterscotch syrup and two scoops of French vanilla.

Still sad, Dylan pulled the white duvet over her head and squeezed her eyes tight, but the tears wouldn't come: they were like the last bag of potato chips stuck in the vending machine—no amount of shaking could make them fall.

This trip was supposed to offer respite from insecurity, and here she was, shades drawn in the South Pacific, wondering if she should ask for lipo or a personality transplant for her next birthday.

Outside, the palm fronds waved gaily in the soft breeze. Young lovers crunched along the snaking seashell path, marveling at the cloudless sky and the singsongy calls of the island's tropical birds. They argued playfully over who was cuter, who had the better spa treatment, who was more deeply tanned, who had a better lunch. These achingly cheerful snippets of conversation seeped though the walls of Dylan's bungalow and stabbed her heart like invisible daggers. All she could do was hate-punch her pillow and pray for a hurricane.

More than anything, Dylan wished her jasmine-scented mom were around to make up a story about how she'd once been dumped by a hot tennis fanatic too. But right now Merri-Lee was in talk show–host mode, getting coverage of today's matches. And maybe even breaking Svetlana and J.T. as the hot It couple of the Open. Dylan could see it now; their toned and tanned arms around each other, smiling for the paparazzi and inspiring made-for-TV movies.

Now what? Fly home? Or do what a Dove soap user would do and drag herself out of bed, hold her head high, and strut across the resort like she hadn't just gotten double-crossed and humiliated? The problem just seemed too big to remedy—like global warming.

Dylan considered calling Massie for advice. But that would mean admitting J.T. had chosen Svetlana over her, and who wanted to say *that* out loud?

Instead, she burrowed under the covers to wait for a revelation . . . or room service. Whichever came first.

Dylan stretched her arms toward the bungalow's thatched ceiling, her limbs finally able to move without aching. Apparently the Motrin plus nineteen-hour nap had done the trick. Now the only muscle still feeling the effects of the Svetlana Way™ was her heart. And wallowing was no longer acceptable. Feeling depressed in paradise was like wearing suede boots in the rain. It was just plain wrong. Besides, she was stahr-*ving*.

She padded over to the stainless steel mini-fridge in the kitchen. A half-full Styrofoam cup of spirulina green detox and a hunk of moldy Havarti stared back at her.

She pulled open the white Formica cabinets.

"Thank Gawd." She reached for an orange box of Wheaties. An action shot of Svetlana midserve graced the front, and Dylan instinctively whipped the box into the sink. She was starving—not stranded.

Feeling empty in a way that had nothing to do with her rumbling belly, Dylan realized she could either sit in her suite or she could move on—preferably to somewhere that had a hearty brunch menu.

She spun around on her tennis-callused heels and marched across the cool black-and-white marble to her walk-in closet. Unzipping one of her many unpacked, color-ful-clothes-containing Louis Vuittons, she grabbed a pair of electric blue drawstring linen pants and a matching Calypso tunic. Kicking her Nikes to the back of her closet, she pulled out her silver platform Havaianas, shocked to realize that her pedicure had barely touched sand since she arrived. Suddenly, a tingle shot up her spine. Now that she was back to being Dylan Marvil, tennis hater, she could do all the things she had missed out on. Tanning, swimming, eating, spa-ing, and getting fashion inspiration from something other than a hard-boiled egg.

Donning round black sunglasses large enough to make Nicole Richie jealous and a black floppy Chanel hat covered in gold C's, Dylan presented herself to the mirror.

"Eight point five."

She spritzed some Clinique Happy perfume, hoping the uplifting citrus-y scent would give her that final boost she needed to face her public. It did.

Once at Béarnaise, the spa's five-star restaurant, Dylan force-smiled at the relaxed guests and strolled along the buffet, alternating between revenge plots and breakfast options. Her mouth watered at the sight of golden brown pancakes, fresh whipped cream, and silver-domed trays loaded with glistening breakfast meats. Pastries, bagels, muffins, and seafood omelets stared back at her, begging to be chosen like scrawny guys during a schoolyard kickball draft.

A long communal table on the sun-soaked patio was the only way Dylan could avoid the depressing table-for-one exchange with the hostess. So she grabbed the last open seat. Moms in various patterned sarongs occupied the other seven. They were already on their second round of coffees and well into their morning gossip session.

"Of course I saw it, Jayna," said Red and Orange Paisley Sarong as she dumped a spoonful of muesli into her collagen-enhanced mouth. "It was so embarrassing."

Her heart racing at full speed, Dylan turned away and gazed out at the cliffs. She scrolled through the mental image of her humiliating tennis match, wondering if anyone had been hiding out with a video camera.

"I'm telling you, if the Academy gave Oscars for 'acting during an interview,' she'd win a truckload," noted Jayna, lifting her glass of fresh-squeezed papaya juice. "All that fake sweetness. It makes my blood sugar rise just thinking about it."

"They should call her Splenda, not Svetlana," added Brown and Yellow Batiked Sarong.

The ladies cackled with delight. Dylan sighed with relief. This was about Svetlana's *Daily Grind* interview. Not her.

"Well, the ball girls didn't buy her public apology," announced Green and Blue Striped Sarong as she wave-asked the waiter to refill her cup of Kona.

"I think it's wonderful that they've all suddenly come down with the 'Russian flu,'" Jayna giggled. "Who says young people don't get involved in politics?"

Wait! The ball girls were on strike? What else had Dylan missed during her nineteen-hour nap?

"Serves her right," Brown and Yellow insisted. "Get it? *Serves?*" She cackled.

Dylan joyfully buttered her Belgian waffle. It turned out she wasn't the only one out to get Tennis the Menace. But she was the only who knew how.

When Dylan volunteered to be the only ball girl for the Women's Final, the ITA chairwoman hugged her for an entire minute. Playing fetch wasn't Dylan's idea of fun, nor was changing back into her tennis whites. But it got her where she needed to be—on the court with Svetlana during her big comeback game.

Thanks to Winsome, Dylan took the court in a drop-waist skirt covered in hand-embroidered hearts to show the world she still had hope. Her scoop-neck tank showcased her now-toned arms, and the built-in boob shelf had just enough padding to turn her A-cups into A-pluses.

She paced the baseline, the focal point for hundreds of spectators and dozens of TV cameras, charged by the daring nature of her plan.

After a sweltering forty-five-minute delay, Svetlana stepped onto the court. She bowed humbly, graciously accepting the outpouring of love from her cheering fans. Dressed in a white tuxedo vest top, super-short satin shorts, and a fierce squint, she looked *Maxim* hot and *Sports Illustrated* determined.

Seconds later, perky newcomer and fellow redhead Lauren Shirley bounced onto the court. She was greeted with a smattering of applause, making it clear she was hardly the main attraction.

The game started, and Svetlana began annihilating her opponent from the word *go*. Dylan sprinted for each stray ball, speedily removing it so the match could continue at its dizzying pace. But still, despite her hair-tossing, sighing, and occasional throat-clearing, Svetlana didn't seem to notice her. And if she did, she seemed the opposite of threatened. At this point, the only thing this revenge plot had to offer was a bad case of shin splints and sweaty pits.

Svetlana won her game, and the crowd cheered like football fans, ah-bviously suckers for a good anger-management comeback story. J.T.'s forehead was practically mashed up against the tinted glass of his family's box. He was holding Boris, wiggling one of his gray paws so it would look like the kitty was waving.

From a distance, he didn't look quite as ah-mazing as she remembered. His pretty-boy features were still intact, but they didn't twist her gut her like they once had. The spell had been broken—not because he'd double-crossed her, but because he'd chosen Svetlana. And even though she was beautiful, toned, and world famous, that didn't mean she was a better catch. The only thing it proved was that J.T. was a tennis stalker with a soft spot for psychos. And that was a major turnoff.

It was time for the players to change sides. Despite Lauren's horrible score, she smile-waved at her mini cheering section as she passed. Svetlana ignored the crowd, her head hung low as if focused on the tips of her sneakers.

"Nikeeee," Dylan burped as Svetlana approached the baseline.

She stopped suddenly, her I'm-in-the-zone squint quickly morphing into wide-eyed surprise. Her expression said, "What are you doing here?" while her blue green eyes scanned the court for some sort of explanation. When she didn't find one, she drew back her racket, ever so slightly, to remind Dylan that she'd tooth-bashed once and wasn't afraid to do it again.

Dylan mouthed, "Whatevs," but her gums tingled with fear.

On the court, Svetlana took the fourth set with little effort, and Dylan was there to pick up every ball. At first she chalked it up to revenge adrenaline, but as her legs sprinted back and forth, she realized that tennis boot camp had left her in pro shape.

Merri-Lee gave her a proud smile from the press box, and Dylan beamed. Her mother had noticed her. In a resort filled with genetically perfect tennis superstars, her mother had noticed *her*! It was a moment fit for a Dove commercial. And it gave Dylan the push she needed to stay the course and finish what she'd started.

"Looks like Sizesix Pimple has finally found her calling," Svetlana hissed when Dylan handed her two service balls.

"And you've finally met your match," Dylan countered, wishing Massie had been there to applaud her speedy comeback.

"I certainly have." Svetlana blew an air kiss to J.T., who annoyingly caught it and stuffed it in the pocket of his white loserfan shorts.

Almost instantly, Svetlana refocused on the game and

began pacing the baseline like a caged lion. *"Huuu-agh!"* She tossed up one of the balls up and smashed it right into the net.

"Let!" the line judge yelled, indicating that Svetlana got a do-over.

Perf! Suddenly, Dylan had the amazing opportunity she'd been waiting for.

Bounding to retrieve the ball, she skipped past Svetlana and whispered, "You're on fire!"

Ignoring the jab, Svetlana pulled a ball out of her pocket and gave it a bounce. It appeared as though she hadn't heard the forbidden compliment. And then she began running in place—a dead giveaway that she had.

The Svetlana Way™ suggested psyching out your opponent with a Sudden-Burst-Of-Energy Jog™ when you were feeling weak. And since Lauren wasn't exactly threatening Svetlana, it meant Dylan was.

Pop!

Svetlana served an ace.

Hmmm.

She wound up again.

"Doing great, Svet!" Dylan flashed the thumbs-up sign while she ran to the other side of the court to retrieve the ball.

Pop! Swoosh. Svetlana served the next ball straight out of the stadium. There was a loud thump, then the whine of a car alarm. The crowd ooh-ed louder than usual.

Svetlana's nostrils flared as she missed not one, not two, but *three* of Lauren's next service points. The crowd murmured and shifted uncomfortably in their metal seats.

Finally, a volley began, and it seemed Svetlana was getting her juice back.

It was now or never.

"You rock, Svetlana!" Dylan whisper-hissed as she crouched along the sideline.

Svetlana glared at her, but Dylan refused to let that trip her up. She had a mission and had to stay focused.

"Great form!" Dylan air-clapped as Svetlana swung back to return one of Lauren's speedballs.

Pop . . . right into the net.

"You're still the best!" Dylan said just loud enough for Svetlana to hear as she ran to retrieve the ball.

"E-nuffff!" Svetlana smashed her racket onto the court.

Dylan immediately backward-jogged to the sideline. But she wasn't fast enough. Svetlana grabbed a ball out of her skirt pocket and whipped it at Dylan's calf. Hard. Then Svetlana chucked another, and another . . .

Cameras started clicking, and reporters rushed the court. Resort security pulled up on golf carts, and Svetlana's mom-coach rose out of her chair. Still, Dylan managed a smile—done, done, and done! She danced around the court as Svetlana pelted her.

"Svet!" Lauren raced around the net to try and stop her, but Svetlana just grabbed Lauren's racket and used it to smash more balls at Dylan. Luckily, the rainbow ball drill and a sixth-grade obsession with *Dance Dance Revolution* had taught Dylan a thing or two.

When a ball came right, she'd jump left. When one came

left, she'd jump right. Forward, back, side, side . . . it turned into a fun little spectacle that had the crowd cheering and the calories burning. The cameras turned to her again. But Dylan hardly noticed. She just kept avoiding balls and giggling, feeling like her old self again.

"Svetlana, stop!" J.T. suddenly appeared, clutching Boris with one hand and trying to wrestle the titanium racket from her grip with the other.

Dylan's insides soared. He *did* care about her after all.

"The *match* . . ." he pleaded. "You're gonna blow it!"

It took all of Dylan's willpower not to pick up one of the balls at her feet and whip it at his face. Then she realized it had never been Svetlana she was competing with for J.T.'s attention. It was *tennis*.

"Get offa me, Loserfan!" Svetlana swung around and smashed her racket into J.T.'s perfect face.

"OWWWW!!!" He dropped Boris. Blood began to gush from his nose, adding a much-needed splash of color to his boring white outfit. A swarm of paramedics raced to his side.

"Find my Boris!" Svetlana pleaded. But nobody tried to stop the gray kitty cat with the haunting blue eyes as he dashed off across the court in search of a normal life.

"SVETLANA!" Mom-Coach tried to grab her, but security arrived first. A cluster of stocky men in Hawaiian shirts and white slacks dragged her off the court.

Of course she kicked and screamed and threatened them in her mother tongue, but all they did was smile dutifully for the paparazzi, as if they were hauling Britney Spears back to Promises.

Dylan was looking on with pride when she noticed Svetlana squirm away from the guard and reach under her white tennis vest. In a flash, she turned back toward Dylan. Security tightened their grip, but it was too late. One last yellow ball shot out from her hand and hurled toward Dylan's brow bone. The crowd, the cameras, the anxious announcers . . . everything seemed muted. The only sound Dylan heard was the *whoosh* of the ball as it Matrix-sliced through the air. Without a single thought, Dylan opened her palm and caught it.

"Aggghh!" It was like getting high-fived by a burning whip. The impact nearly took her wrist off.

The crowd erupted in cheers.

For her. Finally, they were cheering for her!

Dylan transferred the ball into her left hand and shook the pain away.

"Ball girl! Ball girl! Ball girl!" The chant grew.

As usual, Merri-Lee was barking orders at her camera crew. But instead of directing them toward Svetlana, she told them to focus on her daughter.

Dylan blew kisses. She waved. She smiled. She cried.

"Ball girl! Ball girl!"

Fans tossed flowers, teddy bears, and even a few phone numbers written on ketchup-stained Svetlana programs.

After a few minutes, the noise died down, but one voice kept chanting. It belonged to a boy.

A very, very cute one.

The arena was empty now except for Merri-Lee and her staff, who had built a charming little interview set in the center of Court One. The cleanup crew had been ordered to leave her daughter's flowers and teddy bears exactly where they landed, because Merri-Lee thought it added ambiance. Dylan happily agreed.

"This is Merri-Lee Marvil for *The Daily Grind,* coming to you live from the Aloha Open with this year's men's champion, Brady Erickson. He's an amazing player, and quite a heartthrob." Merri-Lee gave her audience a flirty wink. "Congratulations on your big win."

"Thanks, Merri-Lee." Brady swung the Aloha trophy like a beer stein with his beyond-ripped arms. His dark wavy ponytail was partially stuck to his salty, sweaty neck in that ah-dorable Gatorade commercial sort of way. And his chocolate brown eyes, which kept wandering over to Dylan, made her feel sauna-warm. They seemed kind and sincere and . . . honest—qualities she'd never sensed in J.T.'s flashy electric blues.

"This is your first time out of the juniors and into the men's draw. And you won. What's it like being the youngest male to take the Aloha Open?" Merri-Lee crossed her cocoa butter–slicked legs, revealing a pair of tanned calves that had obviously spent the better half of the week on a surfside chaise.

"I just got out there and made my shots. Cartwright played an awesome game. He had me on the run in that first set, but I just dug deep and came up lucky, I guess."

Modest.

"This puts you within striking distance of the tennis gods, Federer and Nadal. What's next?"

"Honestly?" He smiled with a trace of guilt. "I'd like to take a short break from tennis and enjoy Hawaii. Maybe even try one of those butterscotch sundaes everyone is ordering by the pool." He licked his cherry-red lips.

Dylan slid off the director's chair and inched a little closer. Was this guy for real or just an Adam Brody look-alike robot with muscles that had been programmed to say all the right things?

She stared at him with shock and awe. He stared back, nodding, ever so slightly, assuring her that her suspicions were right—he *was* perfect. The intensity of the moment made her stomach lurch in a good way.

"So, *Brady*, what do you do in your free time?" Merri-Lee ech-hemmed, indicating this was not the first time she'd asked him.

"Oh, sorry," he snicker-blushed. Several of the crew smiled too. "I, um, I love hanging out with friends, eating, laughing, and rock climbing."

Well, three out of four isn't bad.

Re-glossing her lips, Dylan felt a surge of self-anger. If only she had noticed his hawtness earlier, she never would have wasted her time on . . .

She shook the thought away. It wasn't *her* fault. She had always been a sucker for packaging. And J.T., with his caramel locks, was shinier.

Merri-Lee leaned into the tennis champ. "I can't let you go without asking this. You've been on the tour with Svetlana since you were both tiny tennis tots. Do you think the ITA made the right move in banning her from the sport until further review?"

Rubbing her still-sore hamstring where one of Svetlana's well-placed shots had nailed her, Dylan wished *she* could answer that question.

He shrugged. "Last time I checked, tennis was not a contact sport, so yeah."

His publicist, a short-haired brunette with black plastic–framed glasses and not enough makeup, folded her arms across her chest and huffed. Then she gave him a deadly I-canNOT-believe-you-said-that glare.

Brady shrugged unapologetically and mouthed, "Well, it's true."

Dylan was officially back in summer-crush mode—v. 2.0.

"One last question." Merri-Lee hooked a chunk of burgundy hair behind her diamond-studded ear. Then she winked at her daughter in a this-one's-for-you sort of way. "Is there a lucky girl who you'll be celebrating with at the ESPN party tonight?"

Gawd! How did her mother know? Was Dylan drooling? Panting? Foaming at the mouth? Not that it mattered. All she really cared about was his answer.

"Well, I'd be the lucky one if I could get the real star of the Aloha Open to do me the honor . . ." Brady extended his hand toward . . . Dylan.

Ehmagawd! Dylan wanted to freeze time. She needed to re-gloss, fluff her hair, nervous-puke, change into something with color, and call Massie to brag. But all she could do was dry her clammy hands on her white skirt and join him under the bright klieg lights.

Where she'd known she belonged all along.

A wonderfully shirtless Hawaiian waiter wearing board shorts and a red and white striped apron slid a smile-shaped bowl down the polished mahogany bar.

"One butterscotch sundae, two spoons," he announced.

Brady's brown eyes widened when the guilty pleasure stopped in front of him.

Without a single self-doubting thought, Dylan grabbed both spoons, loaded them up with gooey ice cream, and stuffed them both in her mouth. "Didn't you order one?" she managed through the onset of brain freeze.

Brady giggle-pulled one of the spoons out of her mouth and stuck it right in his. He didn't even wipe it off.

It seemed like everyone by the pool was envy-staring while Brady and Dylan swapped stories about their lives and friends back home. They were probably wondering what it was like to be highly attractive famous sports icons: BALL GIRL AND RACKET BOY: THE *LOVE* STORY.

"Is this what life without tennis is like?" He licked his lips and dug in deep for another taste. "It's enough to make me give up sports for good."

"Really?" Dylan beamed. "You'd do that?"

Before he could answer, Mom-Coach appeared, her

rectangular head eclipsing the bright sun. Dylan groaned. It was a total Netflix moment—just as the movie was getting good, the DVD broke.

Dylan pulled her black chiffon wrap off the back of her bar chair and draped it over her berry red Juicy one-piece. For some reason, Mom-Coach's chilly stare made her feel exposed.

"Sign, please." The barrel-chested blonde-from-a-box troll slammed a document on the bar. She clicked a fake-gold Parker pen and handed it to Dylan. Everyone on the deck turned to stare.

"What's this?" Dylan inched closer to Brady's strong arms, just in case Svetlana was lurking.

"Confidentiality agreement," she said as though she were chewing chunky beef stew.

"Why would I sign this?" Dylan looked at Brady as if he might have the answer.

"I can have my manager look it ov—"

"No manager!" Mom-Coach stomped her yellow Crocs. "Read and you will understand."

Dylan took another spoonful of ice cream, removed her silver square-framed Marc Jacobs sunglasses, and lifted the document to her heavily mascaraed eyes.

Brady leaned in. He smelled like peppermint from the complimentary special-edition Aveda sports soap in the rooms.

"Confidential!" Mom-Coach pushed him away. "Now read! I have international flight to catch."

Dylan did her best to focus on the confidential, eight-point font on the bright white letterhead. But it was hard, because Brady was inhaling the sundae, and she wanted to get back to both of them before they were gone.

For Dylan Marvil:

Svetlana Slootskyia is sorry for damage caused to you (by her). She is going back to treatment facility to work on anger. When she returns to sport she will emerge with new name and hair color to signify fresh start. Ilana Bravya Slootskyia will be of brown hair with much patience and kindness. And she would like your help. This means no mention of the "episodes" you recorded (twisting wrist and smashing votives). No interviews to talk about how she bashed you with tennis balls. No bad words about her at all. If you do this, we will give you first dibs on all free clothing and merchandise she gets from sponsors for the next ten years. And American Boris when we locate him.

X_____

(Dylan Marvil)

Dylan put a big X through the part about Boris and signed. She knew she could probably ask for more, but why bother? She had everything she wanted.

Now that you're clued in to the confidentiality contract,
you're another step closer to being **IN**.
In the know, that is. . . .

SUMMER STATE OF THE UNION

IN	**OUT**
✓ Purple hair streaks	Summer secrets
✓ Confidentiality contracts	
Euro pop stars	
Shark-tooth necklaces	
Massie & Claire in Orlando	

Five girls. Five stories. One ah-mazing summer.

THE CLIQUE
SUMMER COLLECTION

BY LISI HARRISON

*Turn the page for a sneak peek
of Alicia's story. . . .*

THE CLIQUE
SUMMER COLLECTION

ALICIA

Alicia Rivera stuffed her purple-and-turquoise vintage Pucci silk wrap in the side pocket of her Louis Vuitton carry-on and wheeled it toward baggage claim. She could practically *hear* her mother scolding her for treating the delicate, wrinkle-prone fabric with such reckless abandon. But she opposite of cared. Nadia was back in Westchester and Alicia had just arrived in Spain. Thanks to an all-consuming lipo-gone-wrong trial, her attorney father and supportive mother had to stay home. And that meant *she* was parent-free for the first summer of her entire life.

And the rules were about to change.

The Barcelona International Airport (or *Barth-eh-lona*, as the locals called it) was another reminder that Alicia was a world away from home. Women whizzed passed her, smelling like musky cologne and wearing brightly colored pumps. Men wore hair gel that shined like M.A.C. Lipglass and loafers without socks. College kids with bulging backpacks that had been sloppily stitched with American or Canadian flags shuffled by in Tevas, their expressions a mix of airplane-groggy and let-the-games-begin psyched.

If Massie had been in the overly air-conditioned terminal, she'd have been rolling her eyes at the "poor taste parade."

But Alicia had a secret appreciation for variety. Light denim washes and sneakers that looked like bowling shoes weren't exactly her thing, but they were different—a welcome change from the usual. And wasn't that what summer's all about?

A loud girly squeal, the kind perfected by *High School Musical* fans, forced Alicia's attention to the orange wall of billboards to her left. Between the faded ad for a Goya exhibit at El Prado and some sugary cereal made of red marshmallow–shaped bulls were five Euro tweens giggle-posing next to a poster of an overly Photoshopped, deeply bronzed, hazel-eyed, black-haired boy.

After their picture had been taken, they each kissed his bleached, bathroom tile–like teeth, leaving behind cherry-red lip prints and a citrus-floral medley of the different perfumes they must have been sampling in the duty-free shop.

Alicia stopped in front of the billboard and tried to decipher the yellow all-caps font that shouted: SI ERES UNA VERDADERA BELLEZA ESPAÑOLA TE QUIERO PARA MI PROXIMO VIDEO MUSICAL. EL BAILE RECREADO PARA LA CANCIÓN "RAIN IN SPAIN." LAS AUDISIONES SERAN EN EL HOTEL LINDO. ¡I! TE HARE UNA ESTRELLA.

Alicia had learned enough Spanish from her mother and their six previous visits to know that the pop star on the poster was looking for a real Spanish beauty to be in his new music video. And—from what she could gather—his name was ii!.

Instantly, a vision of herself in a swiveling makeup chair being blushed, blow-dried, then whisked off to wardrobe made her chapped travel-hands slick with excitement sweat. After the Spanish paparazzi had made her a household name, she'd return to U.S. soil ready to claim her seat on the alpha throne. She'd hold a private viewing party in her father's screening room, where the Pretty Committee and their new crushes (TBD) would admire her on the big screen as she played her international music video for them over and over and over. Every time she'd turn it off, they'd beg her to run it again so they could admire her beauty and study her advanced dance moves one more time. It would be the perfect way to start the eighth grade. Massie would envy her times ten. And *that* would give her a surplus of confidence that would fuel her until Thanksgiving, if not a week or two longer.

So what if she wasn't a *real* Spanish Beauty? Her mother was, and that made her half. And *half* of Alicia was better than anyone else's *whole*, at least from what she could see in the airport: Her slick dark hair was the shiniest, her Dior's were the roundest, her navy Ralph Lauren shirtdress and wide gold belt were the most stylish, and her wood-soled Miu Miu wedges were the highest. Besides, she was trained at Westchester's prestigious Body Alive Dance Studios. And there wasn't a purebred in all of Spain who could claim that.

She may not have been an alpha yet, but becoming a Spalpha (Spanish alpha) was totally doable. And once she ruled Spain for a summer she'd have enough experience to dominate OCD. From the moment Alicia stepped off the plane, twenty-seven people—wait, make that twenty-eight—had checked her out. And she hadn't even arrived at baggage claim yet.

When she did, she spotted her sixteen-year-old twin cousins,

Celia and Isobel Callas, sitting in one of those long golf carts used to transport luggage, teasing the driver by repeatedly knocking off his black patent-leather cap. They threw their long, tanned necks back and cackled as he feigned frustration. It probably wasn't every day—or every decade, even—that the pint-sized porter had two leggy, raven-haired socialites ravage him for free. The scene made Alicia's exfoliated feet tingle with joy.

"Yippeeee!" Celia—or was it Isobel?—hollered as she tossed the driver's cap like a Frisbee. It landed on the moving conveyor belt and began making its circular journey. He rolled his eyes playfully and hopped off the cart to chase after it. Isobel—or was it Celia?—jumped in the front seat, gripped the wheel, slammed her metallic gold espadrille on the gas pedal, and began doing doughnuts across the shiny beige floor. Alicia couldn't have been more proud to call them family.

"*A-lee-cia! A-lee-cia!*" they shouted as they sped toward her.

"*Hola!*" Alicia beam-waved, then jumped out of the way. They screech-stopped in front of her, leaped out, and planted a series of double-cheek welcome kisses on her blushing face.

"So great to see you, cousin," said Celia, tugging the massive gold *C* on her massive gold chain. It hung below her barely there cleavage and knocked against the stiff edges of her fuchsia denim vest. She wore it with a burnt-orange taffeta bubble skirt and lace-up gold sandals. Her hair was slicked into a tight bun that reflected more light than the porter's patent-leather cap. "You look very stylish."

"*Grassy,*" Alicia chirped, putting her new abbreviation for *gracias* straight to work.

"I love how you say '*grassy*'! May I borrow?" asked Isobel, who was wearing a Mediterranean-blue tube top, white short-shorts, and oversize blue-plastic-frame Ray-Bans.

They made those?

"*You* can borrow grassy, Iso—I want to borrow that gold belt." Celia reached out and poked Alicia's braided Ralph Lauren belt.

"Given." Alicia smiled, thinking of her new summer wardrobe and how much her cousins were going to worship it. "My closet is your closet, but . . ." Her voice trailed off as she remembered their thirteen-year-old sister, Nina, and her passion for stealing designer clothes.

The Spanish Loser Beyond Repair had spent a couple of weeks at OCD last semester and had not only tried to steal the Pretty Committee's boyfriends but also half of the girls' wardrobes. So far there was no sign of her. Alicia crossed her French-manied fingers and prayed it would stay that way for the entire summer. Hopefully she'd been shipped off to a reform school for kleptomaniacs, because there was nothing less Spalpha than a SLBR tagalong with theft issues.

A loud, New York Stock Exchange–type bell rang, then bags started to appear on the conveyor belt. One by one, they floated by like pageant contestants, sporting pink bows, plaid scarves, and neon tags to ensure they'd be safely reunited with their loving owners. But no one turned to claim them. Instead, the weary travelers could not take their eyes off the three dark beauties and their bright summer clothes. Already Alicia could feel her Spalpha stock rising.

Isobel lifted her blue Ray-Bans, narrowed her almond-shaped brown eyes, and turned to Celia. She said something quickly in Spanish to her sister. Alicia only managed to pick up the words "borrow," "cousin," and "audition." Determined to make this a no-secrets summer, she spoke up:

"Are you talking about the video audition?" she asked, proud that she was already in the know.

"*Si,*" Isobel lowered her voice and her glasses.

Alicia forced a smile, while her dream of becoming a Spanish star collapsed like a snaking wall of dominoes. How was she supposed to compete with the gorgeous-times-two twins?

"Your American clothes will be perfect for the audition," Celia offered.

"I heart that." Alicia rocked back and forth on the wood heels of her Miu Mius. She felt beautiful and bouncy, like her entire body was made of Pantene-commercial hair. "And maybe I can try out in some of your—"

"You can't!" Celia snapped, her gold necklace swinging back and forth. "You are not true Spanish."

"Puh-lease!" Alicia rolled her tired brown eyes. It was bad enough when Massie called her Fannish (fake Spanish) just because her father, Len, was American. But it was quite another thing to hear it from her own flesh and blood. And no self-respecting alpha would stand for it. The old Alicia would have admitted defeat and resigned herself to a summer of cheering on her cousins while she envy-watched from the sidelines. But the new Alicia was going to fight for her rightful place in the alpha kingdom. And she was going to win.

"They asked for a true Spanish beauty, right?" Alicia pressed.

The twins nodded, barely noticing as the porter snuck up behind them, reclaimed his cart, and sped off.

"Well, what I don't have in *Spanish,* I make up for in *beauty.*" Alicia tossed her hair. She was acting the part now—soon she would become it.

"Point," Isobel nodded, still using Alicia's expression from last summer.

"I say we sneak out of the house tonight and go to the Hotel Lindo. We will party there and search for ii! and his entourage and—"

Sluuuurppppp. Sluuuurppppp.

The sound of someone straw-draining the last drops of liquid from a glass bottle put an instant hold on their scheme session. Alicia turned to see why and came face-to-face with Nina, who had been lurking behind her, an empty Orangina in hand. She was still tall and thin. Her boobs were still massive. But she no longer posed a physical threat, thanks to her new hair-*don't*. Thick platinum bangs and a bowl-bob grazed her rounded jaw. On a supermodel in New York who only wore skinny jeans, tight black turtlenecks, and matte red lipstick, this look would have been hawt. But on someone wearing a ketchup stained turquoise racer-back tank with yellow linen pants, it came off like more of a dare.

"*Hola,*" Nina hissed, offering no embrace. She was obviously still bitter that the Pretty Committee had publicly busted her at the OCD Valentine's Day dance for stealing their stuff. They'd then had the police escort her off campus and dump her at the airport.

"*Hola*," Alicia responded coldly. In the split second since Nina had appeared, it seemed like everyone who had been watching them turned away. She was terrible for business.

"I know what you were talking about." Nina rubbed her heavily lined brown eyes like she'd just woken up, smudging blue kohl under her bottom lashes. "But no one has ever seen ii! in person. What makes you think—"

"Go get Cousin's bags." Celia stomped her gold sandal. "*Ándale!* Papa is waiting in the car."

Nina chucked her bottle in a metal trash can and stormed off to retrieve the only set of Louis Vuitton suitcases in the mix.

Isobel leaned in toward Alicia, surrounding her in the unmistakable scent of Bobbi Brown's Beach. "We must not let her know what we are up to. She is a—how you say . . . tag-along! And will make us look bad in front of ii!. If you want to have fun with us this summer, you must avoid Little Sister."

"No prob," Alicia sighed, relieved that they were all thinking the same thing.

"Ready?" Nina asked, wheeling two brown-and-gold suit-cases, one in each hand. She led the way through the sliding glass door outside to the pick-up area.

It was humid and sunny. The foreign smell of cigarette smoke and exhaust fumes wafted around them, reminding

Alicia that she was entering an alternate universe where anything was possible. Betas could become alphas, Fannish could become Spanish, and Nina and her "rob hobby" could be easily avoided.

Suddenly, Nina stopped walking. She turned around and smiled her toothy Julia Roberts grin at Alicia. "Did my sisters tell you we're sharing a room this summer?"

Celia and Isobel quickly turned to face each other, as if they were deeply involved in a telepathic conversation and couldn't be interrupted.

Alicia's heart thumped to the beat of the salsa music blaring from a blue MINI Cooper that had just passed them. "What do you mean? I always get my own—"

"Mama is renovating the guest wing." Nina licked her puffy lips with delight. "So we will all be together. You, me, my graphic-novel collection, and your precious American clothes." She winked.

"Wait! *What?*" Alicia checked her pink, crocodile-strap Gucci watch, wondering if there was time to catch the last flight back to JFK.

Just then, Nina rolled one of the suitcases through a steaming brown clump of . . .

She stopped to examine the stinky wheel. "Uh oh, *perro* poo!"

Celia and Isobel gasped while Alicia buried her face in her hands, knowing exactly how her poor Louis felt.

THE CLIQUE
SUMMER COLLECTION
BY LISI HARRISON

ALICIA 6/3/2008

MISSION SPALPHA:
SPANISH ALPHA!

Alicia's excited-times-ten to discover that Spain's newest pop sensation—¡i!—is searching for a true Spanish beauty to star in his next music video. If she wins the coveted spot, Massie will never call her Fannish (fake Spanish) again. But her *muy* hawt cousins also want in on the video. Can she beat them, or will she have to say adios to her Spalpha summer?

THE CLIQUE

SUMMER COLLECTION

BY LISI HARRISON

KRISTEN 7/1/2008

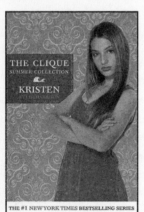

KRISTEN SETS SAIL ON THE LOVE BOAT . . .

While the rest of the Pretty Committee has scattered across the globe, Kristen gets stuck spending her summer landlocked in Westchester. Just when she's about to send out a shore-to-ship SOS to her friends, she scores a job looking after hang-ten hottie Dune Baxter's younger sister, Ripple. Suddenly, Kristen goes from bored to board as she rides the wave of first love. . . .

poppy
www.pickapoppy.com

Available Wherever Books Are Sold

THE CLIQUE
SUMMER COLLECTION
BY LISI HARRISON

CLAIRE 8/5/2008

WILL CLAIRE'S FLORIDA BFFS BECOME *FORMER* BFFS?

Back in Orlando for the summer, Claire is reunited with her Florida best friends after a long year apart. Her FBFFs haven't changed at all. Too bad they think Claire has . . . and not for the better. And when a very special visitor shows up, Claire finds herself torn between Keds and couture. Will Claire finally kiss-immee her past goodbye—once and for all?

poppy
www.pickapoppy.com

Available Wherever Books Are Sold

COMING TO DVD IN FALL 2008

THE CLIQUE
MOVIE

ALWAYS KNOW THE CURRENT STATE OF THE UNION

REGISTER FOR UPDATES AT

THECLIQUEMOVIE.COM

Welcome to Poppy.

A poppy is a beautiful blooming red flower
(like the one on the spine of this book). It is also
the name of the new home of your favorite series.

Poppy takes the real world and makes it
a little funnier, a little more fabulous.

Poppy novels are wild, witty, and inspiring.
They were written just for you.

So sit back, get comfy, and pick a Poppy.

poppy
www.pickapoppy.com